NORTHBOUNDERS

2,186 MILES OF FRIENDSHIP

KAREN LORD RUTTER, Ed.D.

Illustrated by Nathaniel Hinton

Interior Designer: Jovana Shirley, Unforeseen Editing, www.unforeseenediting.com

ISBN-13: 9781511525862

For David, the one who planned the great adventure.

Introduction

Hi! My name is Copper and I am a Golden Retriever who loves new adventures. My very best friend is David, and he plans our adventures. We like to play ball, swim, eat snacks, and take long hikes through the woods.

David likes to take a book when we hike so that he can tuck himself into the nook of a tree and lose himself in reading about things we can do and places we can go. On our walks back home, he tells me all about these magical places.

Through our talks, I've learned about geography, math, history, and science and have gotten a pretty good vocabulary as well.

David uses lots of big words and I have to figure out their meaning. Sometimes, when I arch my brow and look up at him with my big brown eyes, he knows that I don't understand. I call that my "Whaaaaaaaat?" face. He laughs and tells me what the big word means. I like when he talks to me. I listen and learn. You can learn too, just by reading my book.

Well, it's time for dinner, and you've got some reading to do. Enjoy the book, dream up an adventure, and then lace up those boots and explore! You won't regret it.

Map of the Appalachian Trail

BEAUTIFUL
Appalachian
Trail

GEORGIA
TO MAINE

Mt. Katahdin

VERMONT   MAINE

NEW
HAMPSHIRE

MASSACHUSETTS

NEW
YORK

RHODE
ISLAND

CONNECTICUT

PENNSYLVANIA

NEW JERSEY

DELAWARE

OHIO

WEST
VIRGINIA

MARYLAND

VIRGINIA

KENTUCKY

NORTH
CAROLINA

TENNESSEE

SOUTH
CAROLINA

ATLANTIC
OCEAN

Springer
Mtn.

GEORGIA

ALABAMA

FLORIDA

CHAPTER 1
Positivity and Possibilities

Snoozing in the late afternoon sun is my second favorite thing to do. There is a special spot in our house where the sun shines perfectly on the hardwood floor and provides a blanket of sunshine just right for an afternoon nap. I can stretch out on the smooth floor, rest my weary bones, and even do a little snoring if I like.

From my favorite spot, I can listen to the hum of the voices in the house, enjoy the music being played, and sometimes hear the buzz of the bees outside the window. When the window is open, I can hear the rustle of the trees and feel the cool breeze in the spring and the fall. Those are my favorite seasons. Both seasons have perfect weather for my number one favorite activity—exploring the woods and hiking with my best buddy, David.

We love nothing more than heading outside in the early morning and not returning until late in the afternoon. We like to make a game out of deciding the day's snacks and choosing the direction that our day will take us. Freedom to roam and explore is what we both enjoy.

I had hoped that we would have another adventure today. Unfortunately, we won't be going on a walk or enjoying our special snacks since David's best friend, Kristyn is visiting. Kristyn is a great friend, but she doesn't enjoy exploring the woods as much as we do. So, I'm just lying in the sun and listening to their conversation about one of David's newest possibilities for an adventure.

"David, are you really going to hike the Appalachian Trail?" asked Kristyn. "It sounds like that would take a long time."

"The trail is 2,186 miles long, and if I had to guess, I'd say it will take me about 6 months to complete the hike. Some people have hiked it in less than three months, but I think I want to take my time and enjoy it."

"Six months! That's half a year!"

"I know, Kristyn. But I've been thinking about hiking the A.T. for a long time. I've done lots of research and now is the right time.

"That sure is a lot of walking," said Kristyn. "Why not just drive from Georgia to Maine in a car? It seems a lot easier to me. Have you thought about how many pairs of boots it will take to walk through 14 states? Good hiking boots are expensive."

David laughed. "I've been told that I can expect to buy at least three pairs."

"Do you know what to take or what kind of gear you'll need? This just seems like a crazy idea to me!"

"Call it crazy if you want, but can you imagine living every day with just the food and gear you need and the clothes on your back? How nice would it be to see the sun rise and set every day? Can you even begin to imagine how beautiful it will be to see the seasons change right before your eyes and to be able to sleep under the stars?"

"Yeah, and I can imagine the bugs and the snakes and the poison ivy and the bears. I can't even think about my best friend being out there in the wilderness."

"I'll be fine," said David. "I've done a lot of hiking and camping in my lifetime and a lot of reading about hiking the A.T. I also talked to Solo and he has told me all about what I need to take and what I need to be prepared for."

"Who is Solo?" asked Kristyn.

"He's a friend who thru-hiked the Appalachian Trail last year. He has shared lots of information with me and has offered to answer any questions that I have about the trail, hiking gear, and trail food."

"He sure has a funny name. How can you trust a guy with the name Solo?"

David laughed. "That's not his real name; that's his trail name. Hikers are often given trail names by their fellow hikers because of their characteristics or things that happen to them on the trail. Solo got his name because he was hiking alone. His real name is Daniel."

"Well, did Solo tell you that you could get struck by lightning or attacked by a bear or fall off a mountain and die?"

"You worry too much," said David. "I could get killed just walking across the street. Think about the pioneers who came to this country with very little and lived off the land. If they did it, then I can too."

"Well, have you even thought about how Copper is going to feel about being left behind without his best friend for six months? That dog adores you."

"Actually," said David, "I'm thinking about taking him with me."

"What?" Kristyn flung her arms out in exasperation. "So, not only will I have to worry about my best friend, but I also have to worry about my favorite dog getting eaten by a bear and bitten by a snake and falling off a mountain somewhere!"

"You are so dramatic, Kristyn. We'll both be fine. I promise I'll take good care of Copper if his veterinarian says he can go."

Can you believe this? This is definitely the grandest adventure David has ever come up with. He thinks I'm asleep in the sun and not listening, but I heard it all. The best part is that he is talking about taking *me*—Copper—his dog—his best buddy—on the A.T., the Appalachian Trail. He wants to take me on a *long* walk—from here in Georgia, through 14 states all the way to Maine. I'm game. In fact, I can't wait!

CHAPTER 2
Preparations and Perils

It looks like there is a lot to do in preparation for this Appalachian Trail hike. David bought a backpack, a tent, a hammock, rain gear, hiking pants, shirts, and shoes and cooking utensils. Since we will be eating and sleeping outside, he has to be prepared for rain, sleet, snow, and heat.

He's also talking about buying a backpack for me. I will have to take my own food, my dog bowl, my after-dinner treats, my leash, and some water.

But first, I had to go to the veterinarian, so David could receive validation of my excellent health. He needed to hear Dr. Amy say that I could make the trip without health issues. It's silly, I know. Of course I can! We go on a hike every day, don't we? What's so special about this one? If Dr. Amy didn't say I could go, I was going to be mad!

Actually, I like going to see Dr. Amy. She takes good care of me, gives me medicine to get rid of those pesky fleas, talks to me in a sweet voice, and gives me lots of scratches behind the ears.

As Dr. Amy entered the room, she said, "There's old Copper! How are ya, buddy?" She roughed up my fur playfully and then began the exam. She looked at my eyes, my teeth, my paws, and my fur. Then, she ran her fingers down my back, my sides, my legs, and my belly. That's my favorite part because she always gives me belly rubs. This time, Dr. Amy did blood work, checked my urine, checked my temperature, and made sure that I was up to date on my shots. I was extra perfect today and gave Dr. Amy nose kisses in hope of a good report.

Finally, Dr. Amy returned to the exam room and said, "David, the tests came back and everything looks good. Copper is at a healthy weight, his kidneys are healthy, his mouth and gums look good, his blood work looks good and he seems strong".

"He's been hiking with me for years," said David, "but he's never been on a hike this long or strenuous. I just need to be sure he's healthy so that it's okay for him to go."

"My one concern is his age," said Dr. Amy. "He looks like he's about 10 years old, which is equivalent to being a seventy year old man."

"Is that too old for Copper to be walking up mountains, especially considering his arthritis? I think his joints really hurt him sometimes."

"I'll give him a prescription for joint pain, but I think the walking will probably be good for him. Just pay attention and if he seems tired, stop and let him rest. If he seems to be hurting too much, take him off the trail."

"Copper would be heartbroken if that happened. I hope he stays well and gets to finish the hike. Thanks for all of your help."

"Have a great time and send me a postcard to let me know how he's doing."

So yes, I get to go, but I'm concerned about my arthritis too. Sometimes, my joints hurt so bad that walking is very painful. I don't let David see that I hurt because I love our hikes in the woods. Sometimes it is tough being an older dog. My spirit is always willing to go on any new adventure, but sometimes my body decides it's just tired and sore.

Dr. Amy is right about my age. I am 10 years old and getting very close to 11. Neither she, nor David know exactly how old I am because I used to have a different family.

Before I met David, I had a really nice family who took very good care of me. They taught me good manners, played with me, fed me well, and gave me a warm place to sleep. I really loved them.

One night, a huge storm came. The wind was howling very loudly, and the thunder made it sound like the house was being torn apart. Waiting for my family to come home, I huddled in the corner of the house to wait the storm out, but it just got worse and worse.

As I heard the deep BOOM of the thunder and the loud CRACK of the lightning again, I shivered in fear. I found myself panting uncontrollably and pacing back and forth trying to find a way out.

Each time the lightning struck, I recalled my mother lying still in the scarred and smoking soil in the woods. I was just a puppy. I should have known it wasn't real, but I could see the image of her lifeless body curled on the living room floor as if that terrible lightning bolt had struck only moments before. The terror and sadness of that memory coursed through me. I couldn't think straight.

And then I saw my escape. The screen door was right in front of me on the back porch and I knew I could break through if I got a running start. I backed up all the way to the couch in the den, ran through the open back door onto the screened porch, and took a giant leap.

The screen in the door gave way and I was free. I was bleeding, but I was free.

I started running and running and running.

Boom! Crack! Boom! Crack

I had to get away!

I ran and ran trying to get away from the noises and the storm. As I ran, the soaking rain continued to pour and the thunder kept booming and crackling. There was no safe place to hide. Shivering and cold, I had to keep moving to outrun the storm. Just when I thought I couldn't run any longer, I spotted an opening in the earth off in the distance. Turning toward it, I saw that it was a cave and quickly bounded into the darkness. I could smell the rich, dry earth and see the protective walls of the cave which muffled the deafening sounds outside. I scrambled inside out of the rain.

Exhaustion overtook me as I dug a nice bed in the rich warm earth. I snuggled into the hole and quickly fell asleep as the storm continued to rage outside, but I was safe.

When I awoke, I dared myself to peer out into the beam of light making its way through the entrance of the dark cave. I stood up, did my usual morning stretch and realized that my body was sore. Really sore. How long had I run?

I braved the walk to the opening of the cave and when I looked outside, the sun glared back at me. The skies were blue, and the earth was dry. The storm had passed.

I realized that I was painfully hungry. I began the long walk back home looking forward to my usual breakfast and my morning snuggles with my family.

Very quickly, I realized that nothing looked familiar. Nothing smelled familiar. Nothing sounded familiar. I was lost.

Using all of my senses, I made my best attempt to get back home. This land looked nothing like where I lived. My land was flat and I could see for miles. This land was high and I couldn't see over the mountains. My land was green with corn and peas and watermelons growing. This land had wildflowers and lots of trees. The trees all looked the same and were so tall that I could barely see the sky through the treetops.

As I continued my long walk looking for home, I realized that there would be no breakfast with my family. Nor would there be any dinner. Things were different now. I was on my own.

Somehow, I managed to find dinner in the woods among the trees. Squirrels make a tasty meal but they are fast and hard to catch. They can leap through the air, land in a tree, and scamper to the top before I barely notice they have left the ground. Rabbits are good too, but they are just as fast. After chasing several and scraping my nose in a collision with a tree, I finally got a bit lucky and caught my dinner. My belly was full, but my heart was empty. I missed my family.

I don't know how long I walked. Days turned into weeks, and weeks turned into months. I was eating off the land, barely keeping up my strength, and constantly searching for home. I tried everything I could to find my way back to them, but my efforts were in vain. I walked and walked through the woods, through lakes and streams and over hills, but never found them.

Eventually I found a place with lots of houses, where people left bowls of food outside. I gave up my endless trekking and made some friends with the wandering dogs of the neighborhood. They seemed happy, but I hardly enjoyed tagging along on their adventures, because I could not stop thinking about my family.

One day when the leaves were brown and orange and yellow, I was walking through the woods and heard a loud BOOM! Thunder? I turned and could just make out a man in a tree. There was a sound of something flailing through the leaves, braying. I turned to spot a deer stumbling away, badly injured. Danger! Immediately, I started to run away as fast as I could. Then, BOOM! Instantly, sharp pain pierced my side. I fell to the ground, bleeding.

I didn't know what had happened at the time, but I can tell you now that getting shot *really* hurts. The man--a hunter--had probably mistaken me, with my brown coat and my instinct to run away, for a deer. I don't think he was sorry about it, though--he never came to see if I was okay.

I lay still on the forest floor for a while before daring to raise my head. When I did, I saw blood on my fur and felt a sharp pain when I moved. In too much pain to stand or move, I lay in the woods and waited to heal or die.

Amazingly, the gunshot had not injured any major organs, but it really hurt where it entered my body. I spent many days lying in a bed of grass and leaves, licking the wound and keeping it clean. That bullet is still in my belly and is a constant reminder to always be aware of my surroundings.

Fall turned into winter and somehow I survived the cold, dark, and snowy days with the help of the neighborhood dogs I had met, who would sometimes leave me small animals they had killed. Living in the woods certainly was a sharp contrast to my cozy bed with my favorite blanket in front of the fireplace with my family.

The snow eventually stopped falling and winter turned into spring, and I was once again moving with the grace and speed I had before my injury. No matter the season and no matter the number of friends I made, I spent my nights dreaming of my family.

CHAPTER 3
Hoping for a Home

On a beautiful spring morning as I was moping through the forest and feeling sorry for myself, I came to a beautiful wildflower-covered meadow where a family was running, laughing and throwing a ball back and forth. It was the same game that my family loved to play with me. They were laughing and talking and teasing one another just like my family used to do. But, it wasn't my family.

They looked nice and friendly, so I decided to take a chance and try to join them. I moved slowly and carefully, wagging my tail so that they would know that I was friendly.

As the woman threw the ball to me, I quickly retrieved it and brought it back to her. She let out a big hearty laugh and said, "Well, well, where did you come from, you big beautiful dog?"

As she rubbed me and scratched my ears, the little girl said, "Mama, that's not a dog! That's a horse!"

The dad picked up the daughter and laughed saying, "He's not a horse, Mikella, but he certainly is a big Golden Retriever."

"Let's give him something to eat," said Mikella. "His ribs are showing."

"That's just like you," said the boy in the family. "You're always hungry, so you think everything and everybody is always hungry too."

"Actually, David," replied the mom to the boy, "I think Mikella is right. He does look pretty thin."

"Come on, dog," called Mikella. "I'll get you something to eat. I know just what you'll like."

The little girl led me to the house, made me come inside, took a bowl from the kitchen cabinet, and spooned up a big bowl of beef stew. She was right. It was just the kind of food that I loved and I was certainly happy to no longer be chasing rabbits and squirrels for my dinner. This tasted divine.

I liked this family and I made sure to remember my manners. My own family had spent a lot of time teaching me good manners and I wanted to show this new family that I was a good dog. I didn't bark, I didn't enter a door unless invited in, I didn't eat until I was told the food was mine, and I stayed right beside this new family when we walked. We played all day long until finally the dad said it was time to go inside.

"Can we keep him?" pleaded Mikella. "He's such a good dog. Please, can we?"

"This dog has a family somewhere." said the dad. "We need to do everything in our power to reunite them. Just think, Mikella. What if this were your dog? Wouldn't you want someone to get him back to you?"

"I guess," said Mikella, pouting. "But, I sure wish he was ours."

At that very moment, I wished that I had made a better decision in earlier weeks. When I had run away from home, I had had a collar around my neck that had my family's name, phone number, and address on it. When I got shot, my body swelled and the collar became too tight around my neck. I rubbed and rubbed the collar against a rock over and over to try to get it looser. My neck became sore and bloody, but eventually, the collar broke and I shook my head to be free of it. When I heard them mention my family, I realized that was a bad decision. No one knew how to find them.

The new family put ads in the newspaper, searched the Internet for people who had lost their pets, made flyers, and called the Humane Society to see if anyone was looking for a Golden Retriever. There was one response to the Internet search and it seemed as though my family had been found. But, when the family asked them to check for white spots on my belly and to call me by my name, they knew I was not the right missing dog. I don't have white spots and my name isn't Champ. It made me feel sad to know that another Golden Retriever was missing his family too.

As we walked through the neighborhood, the new family asked lots and lots of neighbors if they knew me. But, nobody came forward to claim me. We even drove into town so that all the business owners could see me and determine if they knew my family. I already knew that this plan wouldn't work. I had never lived around here, but there was no way to communicate that to the nice people trying to find my home.

I was still really sad about being lost because I missed my family. However, I knew that these people were really nice and were taking good care of me. They had done everything possible to reunite me with my family.

This new family talked about bringing me into their family and discussed whether or not it would be a good idea. They finally realized that I had *already* become a part of the family when Mikella declared, as she nuzzled my neck with her cheeks, "Daddy, I love him!"

"David, what do you think about adding a dog to the family?" said the mom to her son.

"I feel like he is already a member of the family. I feel the same as Mikella does. I already love him and he'd make a great hiking partner."

The mom looked at the dad and he nodded his head in agreement. They wanted to keep me. I had a new family.

"Yes!" squealed Mikella. "Let's go play, dog."

"Don't you think we should decide as a family what his name should be?" asked the dad. "It doesn't seem right to keep calling him *dog*."

"We could call him Bailey," said the mom.

"No," said Mikella. "Everyone and her brother has a dog named Bailey."

David leapt up and said, "I've got it. Since he has such thick copper-colored fur, why don't we call him Copper?"

Mikella jumped up and said, "I love it!"

David's mom and dad looked at each other and nodded appreciatively. "Sounds good to me," his mom said.

"I like it too," said David's dad. "He'll be our Copper Head."

"No, Daddy," said Mikella. "Just Copper, not Copper Head."

"Ok," he laughed. "He'll just be Copper. Now, you and Copper Head go on and play."

Mikella rolled her eyes and then ran off to her room to play with the newest member of the family.

The name fit. I liked it, and I loved my new family already.

This day was the beginning of life with my new family and the beginning of my days spent hiking with David.

CHAPTER 4
Plans and Pitfalls

"Well, buddy, it seems that you are officially going on this Appalachian Trail adventure. I bought you this nice blue backpack, and it is just your size." David roughed up my fur as he teased me and said, "You've got to pull your own weight, you know. There will be no slackers on this adventure."

"I got you these cool blue boots too," laughed David. "Let's try them on to make sure they fit."

He put one little blue boot on each paw and stepped back to look at them.

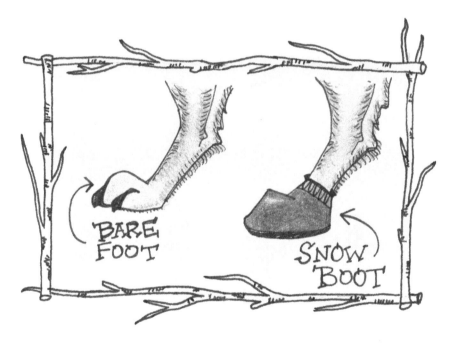

"Yep, they fit just right and they look good with your copper-colored fur. You'll be the coolest dog on the trail."

David put the little boots and a tin of salve in my backpack. The salve will be to protect my paws when we have to hike on sharp rocks. The boots are for protecting my feet in ice and snow.

The boots are made of waterproof cloth and have Velcro straps that close them around my feet. I've never worn boots before, but we are taking them just in case I need them. We have to be really prepared on this hike and I don't mind carrying anything that will help us be successful.

To test the backpack and determine if it fit me well, David filled six quart size bags full of my dry dog food and put three bags on each side of the pack. He was careful to balance out the weight on each side.

Since I am 10 years old and weigh 97 pounds, Dr. Amy suggested that I should not carry more than 15 lbs. in my pack. David put the pack on me and it felt great. He tugged at the straps under my belly and adjusted the pack a few times to try to make it perfect. Then he stepped back to take a look.

"Well, how do you like it buddy? You look like a hiking dog now." laughed David.

I pranced and nuzzled his hand so that he knew that it was a good fit.

To practice for our hike, we would take long walks with our packs on. We would climb mountains, cross streams, go deep into the woods, and walk in open fields with the sun bearing down. My backpack didn't bother me at all. David kept checking it to be sure that it didn't rub my skin, but it was always a good fit and I liked wearing it.

After months of walking in the woods to get in shape for the trip, David prepared a "shake-out" hike to make sure that we had all the right gear, that everything fit well, and that I was up for the rigorous task ahead of us. He said it was called a "shake-out" hike because it would give us a chance to shake out anything that we didn't need or that didn't work as it should. He put all of his hiking gear in his backpack including the tent and cooking utensils, put my supplies in my backpack and off we headed to the North Georgia Mountains. There we met up with two of his friends who also wanted to hike the A.T. in the future.

Our shake-out hike was going really well until our second day in the mountains when the skies turned bright white with a solid bank of clouds, the wind got cold, and it started to snow. It was fun at first, and I jumped and played in it. After a while, though, my paws got really cold. The snow would get stuck between the pads on my paws and I had to stop and bite the snow to get it out. I could clean my front paws, but the backpack kept me from reaching my back paws. Fortunately, David could see that I was having trouble with my feet because I kept stopping. He took out his knife and carefully scraped the frozen snow from between the pads on my paws.

After clearing my paws of snow, out came the blue boots that he had bought for just this occasion. When he put them on my feet, I still didn't really like them. It was like walking on a strange surface and I didn't feel sure footed. I walked slowly and awkwardly at first. David's friends started laughing because I was walking so strangely! They later told me that I was really lucky because I was the only one with snow boots.

As we continued our hike in the snow and rain, we realized that the gear was working as it should and seemed to be exactly what we needed. We had survived extremely cold weather, snow, and rain. We fit perfectly in our tent and there were no leaks. The camping pad kept the sleeping bags off of the cold tent floor and David's zero degree sleeping bag kept us both warm.

I was very comfortable in the tent and slept well. Sometimes I slept under David's legs on his sleeping mat because it was really warm there. Sometimes I slept by his side. Other times, I liked sleeping on the tent floor and having lots of space to myself.

Overall, it was a good trip and good preparation for what was about to come. When we returned home after the shake-out hike, David continued planning how we would cover 2,186 miles of trail between Georgia to Maine.

An A.T. guidebook showed him the distance between shelters where he could spend the night on the trail. These shelters are platform buildings with a roof and open walls which keep hikers from having to carry a tent. The hikers lay their pads and sleeping bags on the platform floor side by side, and hang their packs from the ceiling. This gives hikers some protection from inclement weather.

David also mapped out the towns near the trail so that he could get food and other supplies as we needed them on the hike. He called this task *resupply*.

At one point during the planning process, it looked as though I wouldn't be going on this adventure at all. As David planned his trip, he discovered that dogs are not allowed on the A.T. inside the Great Smoky Mountain National Park in North Carolina.

I was devastated! David wasn't happy either, but he understood that rules are rules and we must follow them.

So, after much deliberation and study, David decided to do what is called a "flip-flop thru-hike". He would start his hike to Maine in the Smoky Mountains without me. He would hike 72 miles through the park by himself. Then, his mom would bring me to join him at the north end of the park, and I could hike the rest of the way to Maine with him. From Maine, we would "flip-flop" back to North Carolina and continue the hike southbound into Georgia. Perfect! I still get to go.

There are many ways to hike the trail. A hiker can do a flip-flop hike, a section hike, or a thru-hike. A *thru-hike* is when someone starts in Georgia and hikes to Maine in a single trip or starts in Maine and hikes to Georgia in a single trip. Those who start in Georgia and hike towards Maine are called Northbounders. Those who start in Maine and walk south are called Southbounders.

NORTHBOUNDERS

A flip-flop hike is when someone hikes north for part of the trail and then flip flops back to the starting point and hikes south on the trail. Or, they can begin the hike going south and then flip-flop to go north.

A section hike is when hikers walk a section of the trail, leave the trail to go back to work, school, or home, and start again where they left off to hike another section at a later time. They repeat this over and over until they have hiked the entire trail. Sometimes, it takes years for the section hikers to complete the trail. David has a friend who section hiked, and it took him twelve years to get to Maine by hiking two weeks every summer. He finally made it. Now, *that* is perseverance.

But we are going to do a northbound flip-flop hike, staying mostly ahead of the crowds who hike northbound each year. When they catch up to us, we'll be northbounders too. David is leaving tomorrow, and in one more week, I'm going to join him. I just hope we're ready.

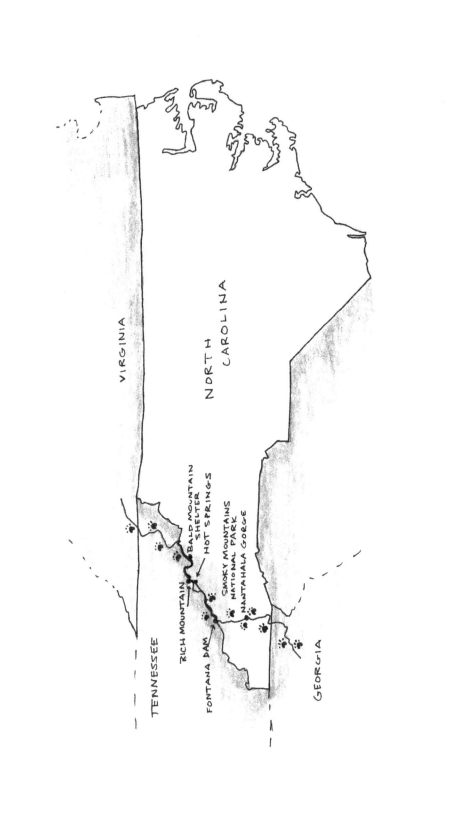

CHAPTER 5
North Carolina News

In mid-March, David left without me to start his hike at Fontana Dam in North Carolina at the southern end of the Smoky Mountain National Park. It took him a week to hike through the park and I really missed him. David's mom took me on long walks just to be sure I stayed in shape and was ready for the trip. They arranged for me and David to meet again just north of the national park in Hot Springs, North Carolina.

We arrived at the meeting point early and waited. When I saw David walking up the trail, I ran as fast as I could and pranced all around his feet. I knew it was bad manners to jump up and put my paws on his shoulders but I just had to get closer to him. David was very happy to see me

He leaned in close, nuzzled next to my face and said, "Hey buddy, I missed you, too". Then he roughed up my fur, gave me a big hug and my favorite ear scratches. A week is a long time without your best friend!

Our hike began with a stroll next to the river and then went straight up the side of a mountain. We went up, up, up and it was really testing my muscles and my strength. Could a 10-year-old dog really do this? We were about to find out.

We finally made it to the top of the mountain, and it was beautiful up there. There were so many good smells and clean fresh air to breathe. We hiked for what seemed like a long time, stopped and had a snack, hiked some more, and then David said, "I think we'll pitch our tent right here on the side of Rich Mountain tonight, Copper." It sounded good to me. So, my first day of hiking ended with a nice meal, a treat, and sleeping beside the ridge of the mountain inside a warm tent.

Before we could sleep, David had to hang our food bags up in a tree to keep bears from finding them and destroying them. Bears have a very keen sense of smell and are very strong. If they smell food, they will find it, rip the backpack open with their sharp claws, and eat the food inside. Mice and squirrels will also chew through the pack to find food.

That's not only bad for David and me since we wouldn't have any food. It's bad for other humans too. Bears begin to associate humans with food. This can be dangerous since bears are much bigger and stronger than humans. Bears know how to find their own food in the woods. They don't need ours. But if they learn that it's quicker and easier to steal a snack from a hiker, every hiker they come across will be in danger. That's why hikers are very careful to keep the woods free of trash and leftover bits of food. Those items would attract bears, raccoons, squirrels, and rats and that would make it very difficult to enjoy a hike.

"Ok, Copper, we've got to figure out how to get our food bags up in that tree so the bears won't get our food."

I knew just what David needed and it was in my pack. I ran over to where he had placed my pack on the ground and pulled the zipper with my teeth. I pulled the pack open and tugged out the rope from my pack.

"Perfect," said David. "Great idea."

David tied the rope to our bags and then tied a big rock to the other end of the rope. He threw the rock end of the rope over a big tree branch, picked up the rock on the end of the rope and began to pull the bags up higher and higher. Then, THUD! The big tree limb broke and came tumbling down and bounced right off his back, nearly knocking him over.

"Ow!" exclaimed David, "I guess these bags are heavier than I thought."

I grabbed onto the rope and tugged it forward, stopped in front of a giant tree, and sat looking back at David. This was the perfect tree.

We went through the same process: tie a rock on the end of the rope, throw the rock over the tree branch, pull on the rock to hoist the food bags on the tree, and secure the rope so they don't tumble back down. This time it worked. Those bears wouldn't be getting *our* food tonight!

Now that the food was secure, we hustled into our tent. It rained all night while we slept, and it was cold! David could see that I was shivering and he reached for me saying, "Come on buddy, come over here under my legs. This sleeping bag will help to keep you warm."

That sleeping bag made a huge difference. I loved sleeping tucked up next to him just as close as I could get. I felt safe, warmer, and content.

When I woke up the next morning, I was shivering uncontrollably. David could see that I was very cold, so he put me in the sleeping bag to let me warm up while he went to collect water from the stream and make breakfast.

David took some time to write in the shelter log before we hiked on. At each shelter, there is a book where hikers leave messages to other hikers or write inspirational messages to keep hikers upbeat when the day has been long and tiring. It is also a way for hikers to learn about news and events of importance to them. Someone may report a bear sighting or post about a found item or find help for a hiker in need. David just drew a small picture of himself being flattened by a falling tree branch and backpack and signed it with both of our names: Blast and Copper.

Blast was the trail name given to David by a hiker in the Smoky Mountains who commented that David always looked like he was having a blast. The name stuck and now David introduces us as Blast and Copper.

I crawled out of the sleeping bag just as David was finishing his drawing, bounding and ready to go. I guess it just takes a little longer for us old dogs to get our bones warm. David smiled, shoved the sleeping bag back in his pack, and strapped my own on my back.

We continued our climb to the top of Rich Mountain. David climbed the lookout tower, which I thought was pretty silly, since it was obviously too foggy to see anything. I waited on the ground. When he came back down, I was itching to see more of the trail. Because I always started out trotting in the morning, David let me lead the way. By afternoon, I would be slowing down, and David would take the lead. We made a good hiking team.

"Good morning!" said a voice from behind us. "Dovetail here. I've been watching that beautiful dog all morning. I was a little worried about finding my way in this fog, so I tried to keep you two in sight."

"Actually," David said, "even in the fog, I've been able to see the white blazes. The trail is really well marked. That white rectangle is a welcome sight. By the way, my name is Blast and this is Copper."

"It's good to meet ya," said Dovetail. "I'll be seeing you again on down the trail, I'm sure. I like seeing Copper out here. It makes me a little less homesick for my own dog back home."

So, *that* explains why David never gets lost on the trail. He looks for white paint known as *blazes* painted on the trees!

As we hiked on that day, the wind began to howl, the snow began to fall, and the temperature dropped below freezing. Walking became harder as the snow piled higher and higher.

We passed another hiker who introduced himself as Hungry Man. It was easy to see how he got *his* trail name. He was happily munching on a huge peanut butter sandwich that he held in one hand while another sandwich waited to be eaten in the other hand. I sidled up to him and edged toward his hand to let him know that I liked sandwiches too.

"Ha!" Hungry Man exclaimed, snatching the sandwich away. "I think your dog would rather stop and eat than keep walking, Blast!"

David nodded. "Yeah, we're both pretty hungry and tired. I think I'm going to stay in a hostel tonight. This snow is getting pretty deep, and the temperature is already below freezing. The weather report says it's going to hit a low of 14 degrees tonight."

"Yeah," said Hungry Man, "I'm thinking of doing the same thing. I heard there's a hostel about a mile off the road crossing just ahead."

We trudged on in the snow with David and Hungry Man talking and looking forward to sleeping in a warm place. After learning that the hostel accepted dogs, we were able to get a room for the night. The hikers had all gathered around a big warm wood stove and were talking about the weather and the trail. Everyone had trudged for hours through the snow and was happy to be warm. I was happy to be curled up at their feet with a special sandwich David had made just for me. The satisfied hikers melted into their seats as the fire began to lull us to sleep.

"Ahhh… this is the life," said Hungry Man. "A warm fire, hiker friends, and a beautiful Golden Retriever to snuggle with."

As the light shone through the window of the hostel the next morning, I could see that it was still snowing and the snow was very deep. Snow made it hard to walk and hard to stay warm. David calls walking in this stuff "*snow blazing*". That means that the snow had completely buried the trail, and it was up to us to find and reveal it by tramping down a foot of snow with each step. The snow drifts were sometimes as deep as four feet, and I was thankful that my backpack served as a sort of snow buoy, letting the piles of snow take some of the pack's weight off of me while I slogged through the snow. I had to wear the snow boots to keep the snow from building up between the pads on my paws again. There was nothing that I could do about the icicles forming on my face, though. I'm sure that I looked pretty silly that day.

David was the leader on the trail because it was just so hard for me to get through the snow. We stopped in a shelter for lunch and since no one was around, David invited me into the shelter to have my lunch out of the snow. He winked at me and said, "It sure is nice to get out of the snow for a while, isn't it, icicle dog?"

After lunch, we slogged on only a couple more miles before it was finally time to stop for the night. David wanted to stay in a shelter, but there were already too many people there. The shelter was filled with backpacks, sleeping bags, and bodies, and there was another group of hikers, equally as large, standing outside.

One of them said, "Hey there, how's it going? Don't think I've met you before."

David replied saying, "My name is Blast and this is Copper."

"I guess that means that you are having a blast out here on the trail. Am I right?"

"I certainly am," answered David. "What's your name?"

"SoFar", he replied.

"Your name implies that you are enjoying the trail *so far*," said David.

"That's right. I'm a bit of a pessimist so I'm only willing to say that I'm enjoying the hike *so far*," he answered.

"That's fair", laughed David. "We never know what lies ahead. Who knows if I'll still be having a *blast* when I get to Pennsylvania, right?"

"Fair point. In fact, who even knows if we'll even be able to enjoy ourselves this very night? The shelter's full and it looks like we're going to have to pitch our tents right here in this snow."

"I agree," said David, "I was hoping to sleep in a shelter tonight, but it's not going to happen."

"Me too," said SoFar. "But, hey, this is a nice open space with room for two tents."

"Sounds good," said David. "I'm just ready to be warm and dry. But, it looks like it's going to be a while before I can clear all this snow to set up a tent."

"I don't have time for all that," said SoFar. "I'm just gonna put my tent right on top of the snow."

And, he did. Minutes later, he was inside his tent and cooking his dinner.

Meanwhile, David cleared a foot of snow from a 6 foot by 6 foot section of ground so that the tent could be on the warm earth. I supervised this production while I ate my supper to ensure it was done properly. The sun was gone by the time David finished digging and started cooking his own supper, but it was a warm night of sleep when the time finally came. We had the earth below us, and the tent walls to keep the wind and snow off of us.

When we awoke the next morning, SoFar said, "Hey Blast, how'd you sleep?"

"Great!" replied David.

"Well, I was freezing all night!" said SoFar with a trembling voice.

SoFar was really shivering. I'm glad that David took the time to dig down to the earth. We were very warm and still dry inside our tent.

David packed up our tent, put his backpack on, strapped me into mine, and we started our journey in the snow again. As we trudged through the snow, my snow boot got stuck and got pulled from my paw. I stopped in the snow, took the boot in my teeth and desperately tried to put it back on. It was no use. The opening was just too small with the Velcro strap in place.

I took the boot in my mouth and tried to catch up with David, but it was too hard to move that quickly through the snow. I dropped the boot and gave a single bark to stop him, but David had his headphones in listening to an audiobook and didn't hear. It was useless. Finally, I gave up and headed down the trail as quickly as I could. As I walked, *that* paw became very cold.

Later down the trail, I heard a voice say, "Dirty Mike here passing on your left. I thought your dog might be needing this in all this snow and ice."

He was holding up my snow boot.

David stopped suddenly, took his headphones out, and turned around, a confused expression on his face. Then, he saw the proffered boot and smiled. "Wow, thanks," said David. "I didn't even know he lost it. Mighty nice of you to bring it along."

"No problem," said Dirty Mike. "See you down the trail."

"That was awfully nice," David said, as Dirty Mike loped away. "I wish he'd given me his name."

He did, *silly!* I thought, shaking my head. *If you'd take your headphones out and pay attention sometimes...*

I was sure glad when David put that boot back on my paw. It was very nice of Dirty Mike to bring it to me, but that's just how these hikers are: they take care of one another.

As we walked on through the day with our goal of a warm shelter for the night, an exciting thing happened for David and the other hikers. At a road crossing where the A.T. has to cross a highway, David shouted, "Trail Magic!"

I had no idea why he was so excited, but then I saw the reason for the excitement. There were big chocolate chip cookies and Mountain Dew sodas in coolers by the side of the road with a note that said, *Keep on hiking and enjoy a little trail magic on me.*

David and the other hikers were very careful to take only one cookie and one soda. They wanted other hikers behind them to enjoy the magic as well. David gave me one of my dog treats so I could join in on the celebration of trail magic.

This little bit of trail magic gave us the jolt we needed to hike on with a little more bounce in our step.

We arrived at Bald Mountain Shelter just before dark and were eager to find a warm spot for the night. Instead we were greeted by a huge snowman and snowballs flying in all directions. The hikers who made it to the shelter ahead of us were certainly enjoying the snow!

"Watch out, Blast!" yelled Dirty Mike as he hurled a big snowball at David.

"Coming right back at ya." yelled David as he grabbed a fistful of snow and hurled it toward him.

This started even more snowballs flying. The hikers, who introduced themselves as Foxfire, Ramblin'Man, Hitchhiker, and Piney, laughed and played and kept adding more items to the snowman.

"Come here, Copper." yelled Foxfire. "I made you a snow cone!"

He had made a nice ball of snow for me and held it while I licked and ate the cold snow. Then he jumped out of the shelter and said, "Let's play, Copper".

I don't know where I found the energy after sloshing through the snow all day, but Foxfire and I played in the snow with the other hikers until we tired of the games. I discovered that *playing* in the snow is much more fun than slogging through it on long hikes.

After the snowball fight, David found a place in the shelter and I found a place nearby to curl up for the night. Just as I was settling in, a girl who called herself only G, said, "David, if it's alright with the other hikers, may I bring Copper into the shelter to snuggle with me for the night? We could keep each other warm."

David said, "I don't mind but you'd better ask everyone else."

David knew the unspoken rule of the trail. Trail etiquette required that all other hikers in the shelter had to agree to allow a dog in the shelter and that the owner should never ask for this permission.

"Can he please come in the shelter and keep me warm?" asked G as the hikers bedded down in the shelter.

"Absolutely!" said Hitchhiker.

"Of course." said Ramblin' Man

"Fine with me." said Piney as she snuggled deeper into her sleeping bag.

G said, "I really like Copper because he is so well behaved. I've met some other dogs on this trail and they need to learn some manners."

"Yeah," said Ramblin' Man, "they bark and jump up in the shelter without an invitation, beg for food, and jump on you. I don't like that. Copper never barks, he never begs for food, he never jumps on you and if you invite him in the shelter, he just comes in and lays down and sleeps".

"He's a good hiking dog. That's for sure." agreed Hitchhiker.

I felt very happy as I nodded off to sleep that night. My manners were paying off and I was making lots of new friends. Who knew that using your manners could have such perks? Instead of sleeping on the cold ground, I found myself snuggled up to a very warm sleeping bag and the nicest girl snuggled inside. She sweetly said, "Sleep warm, Copper," pulled me close, gave me a big hug, and fell asleep. We kept each other warm and snuggly all night long.

We started hiking early the next morning and really enjoyed the sun shining on the trail and warming our bodies. I could tell that the other hikers were just as excited to see the sun as I was even though the sun was turning everything into mud. Sloshing through the mud was much better than sloshing through snow. It felt good on my paws. I was tired of cold snow and I was tired of snow boots!

Notes from the Appalachian Trail in North Carolina

- Always take the time to make your shelter warm in cold weather, even if it means digging down to the earth through ice and snow.
- Humans on the trail look out for one another and their dogs.
- Trail Magic is when someone brings snacks and drinks and places them on the trail so that the hikers have a surprise treat and know that others are wishing them well.
- There is something called trail etiquette. All dogs and hikers should follow it. Dogs are generally not allowed in shelters. But, when one human requests that a dog be invited into the shelter and all other humans agree, a dog can have a very warm and cozy night with new friends.
- Always use your manners; humans like you better that way.
- Food has to be out of the reach of bears and other animals.
- All food scraps have to be picked up on the trail.
- Humans are very concerned about the weather and talk about it constantly.
- A hostel is a house for hikers with beds, a place to shower, and a place to eat.
- It is fun to hear the hikers "trail names" and how they got them.
- David's trail name is Blast. My name is still Copper.
- According to David, we have walked 169 miles so far and completed 8% of the Appalachian Trail.

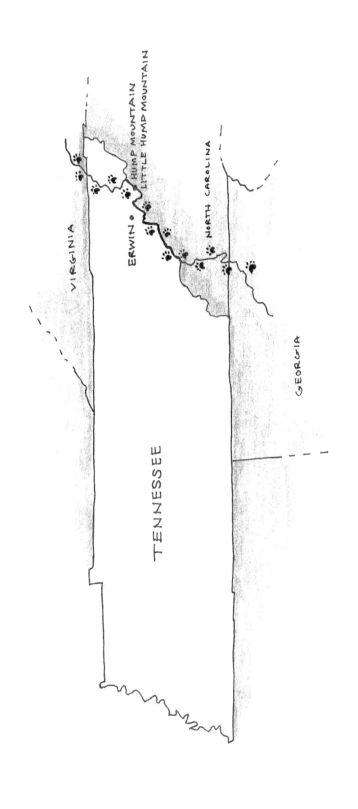

CHAPTER 6
Tennessee Trekking

Two days later, we wrapped up the first North Carolina section with an *easy* six mile *downhill* walk into Erwin, Tennessee. Best of all, it *wasn't* snowing! David had planned to stay in a hostel in Erwin and resupply our food. We arrived fairly early, so we rapidly made new friends: Cricket, her sister Trixie, and her puppy Roscoe. I liked Roscoe and we had fun running around, sniffing all the new scents, chasing the squirrels and frogs and lizards, and lazing in the sun. The following day, we all left together as a group.

While David, Cricket and Trixie hiked together, Roscoe and I could explore some on our own. There were lots of hills where Roscoe and I enjoyed racing to the top. Sometimes he beat me and sometimes I beat him. He's a lot younger and faster, but I had better wilderness intuition and could always find the shortest route to the top.

"Cricket," said David. "Copper and I are going to have to find a water source soon. We're getting low on drinking water. You go on ahead and we'll meet you and Trixie at the shelter this evening."

"Ok, see you there," replied Cricket. "Trixie and I have enough for a couple more days."

Water wasn't plentiful in this area, so carrying water was essential. We stopped at a little brook where David pulled his water pump and filter from his pack and began filling the water bag. The water source didn't look so clear, but it was water, and we were running low.

While David filtered water upstream, I walked downstream and had a nice long drink. It felt so good after our long hike.

Once the water was filtered and tucked away, we began hiking toward the shelter where we would spend the night. I was excited about seeing Roscoe again and was keeping a nice pace with David.

When we finally reached the shelter, I played with Roscoe for a short while, ate my dinner, and then lay down for the night. I couldn't get comfortable because my belly was hurting. At first I thought I'd eaten too much, but this belly ache felt different. It felt like there was something in there pinching me, punching me, and squeezing my stomach. My belly was cramping terribly, and I couldn't ignore the pain.

I tried rolling onto my left side to relieve the pain, but to no avail. Lying on my right side was even worse. Standing up was no way to fall asleep, but it hurt the least of all. I just wanted to curl into a ball and find sleep so that I could forget about how bad I felt. Unfortunately, sleep never came.

While David slept, I spent the night vomiting. What was wrong with me? It kept happening over and over again.

I paced back and forth all night, unable to lay down. As the night drew on, I became weaker and weaker from the constant heaving. My mouth was so dry that it felt like sawdust. I needed water but there was none in sight. The water that David had given me at dinner was long gone. How was I going to survive the night? The dry heaving just wouldn't stop. I didn't want to wake up David, because I was afraid we would have to stop hiking. All night, I worried and tried to fight the pain.

Cricket must have heard my suffering because she got up to check on me just as I thought I couldn't take it anymore. She gave me some water, but the minute it hit my stomach, it immediately came back up. Something was *really* wrong with me. Cricket tried again to give me water with the same result. She decided that it was time to wake up David.

When David got up and saw me, he knew I was a sick dog. He cleaned up my mess and then stayed by my side for the rest of the night. It took a long time before I finally kept some water down, but David never gave up on me.

When morning came, David fixed my breakfast hoping that I was better. The sight of food just made me queasy. I couldn't bear the thought of eating.

When I refused my usual dog food, David cooked a small amount of rice for me in his portable stove to see if I could keep that down. I didn't want any of that either, but I knew that if I didn't *try* to eat, David would think I was too sick to continue. I didn't want to stop hiking. I just wanted to get better and keep moving toward Maine.

I stood up, still feeling exhausted, but managed to take a few steps toward the trail.

David said, "Copper, let's try to get you walking and see if that helps you. We'll go slow and steady until you feel better."

We began to hike slowly up the hill with David keeping a watchful eye on me and constantly giving me water. He knew that I felt terrible, but he also knew that I would need medicine to help me get well. The only way to find help was to keep walking. I managed to slowly trudge through the day, throwing up several times along the way and eating every patch of melting snow that we passed, desperately trying to keep down some water.

David reached down, patted my head and said, "We have to keep going, buddy. We need to find you a doctor."

That day, I walked nine miles on an empty stomach, climbing both Hump Mountain and Little Hump Mountain. The mountains were long and tiring to climb, but it felt better to walk than to stop. David stopped to check on me every mile, but we finally made it to another hostel, where I was invited to stay in the bunkhouse. I immediately lay down and fell asleep. Dinner was of no interest to me.

David had called a veterinarian after we arrived at the hostel and found that he made house calls. He stopped by to examine me, and I overheard David discussing my symptoms.

"Copper has been throwing up since last night, and he's had bloody diarrhea. I hated to make him walk today, but I knew he needed to see a doctor."

"Has he been drinking water?" asked the veterinarian.

"Yes, but most of the time it came back up."

"I'm pretty sure that he has a case of Giardiasis. It is caused by a parasite usually found in contaminated streams or soil. Copper has all the classic symptoms: vomiting, diarrhea, listlessness, and lack of appetite. You did the right thing by making sure he drank lots of water. That's how he was able to hike those last miles with you. He can live without food for a few days, but not without water. He'll want to eat again as soon as we can get some medicine into him to kill the giardia and let him rest."

He pronounced the name of this mean little parasite like "gee-are-dee-a" and said I probably got it from drinking from that dirty stream where David filtered his water. I didn't really care what it was called, I just wanted it gone.

The veterinarian told David to watch me, to make sure I drank water, and got a full five day course of the medicine which would take care of my illness.

David knew that I needed to take the next day off to recover and he paid the owner of the hostel for another day's stay. The owner really liked me so she came up with a plan to help me get some rest and keep David hiking.

"Blast," she said. "I know that you only have a limited amount of time to hike the trail, and it could take Copper a few days to get over his sickness. Why don't you leave your backpack here with me? You could just take some food and water with you and slackpack for the next few days. I'll drive you about 10 miles up the trail and you can hike back to here. That would give you ten more miles toward your goal and give Copper time to recover."

"That's a great idea. Copper will appreciate it; he seems to really like you. Thanks for the offer. I accept."

I did appreciate her kindness because I knew I had to rest to get better. I just didn't want David to get used to hiking without me. He already thought that I may be too old to hike this trail and I didn't want him to get any thoughts about me not being strong enough to continue.

Thankfully, the time off and the medicine worked their magic. David slackpacked for two days, hiking 20 more miles of the trail. On the third day, I was ready to go. I woke up to the sun shining, my stomach feeling good, and a wonderful breakfast waiting for me. I made a mental promise to David that I would never drink nasty water again and that I would not be sick on the trail for the rest of the hike.

Notes from the Appalachian Trail in Tennessee

- Giardia is a parasite that can live in water, on soil, and on food. It can make humans and animals very sick. This is why David filters all of the water he gets from streams and rivers before he drinks it.
- David does whatever it takes to help me stay well including obtaining medicine if I need it.
- I don't like being sick!
- Slackpacking means that David hikes with only food and water and leaves the big heavy 30 pound backpack behind with a trusted friend.
- We have walked 282 miles and completed 13% of the Appalachian Trail.

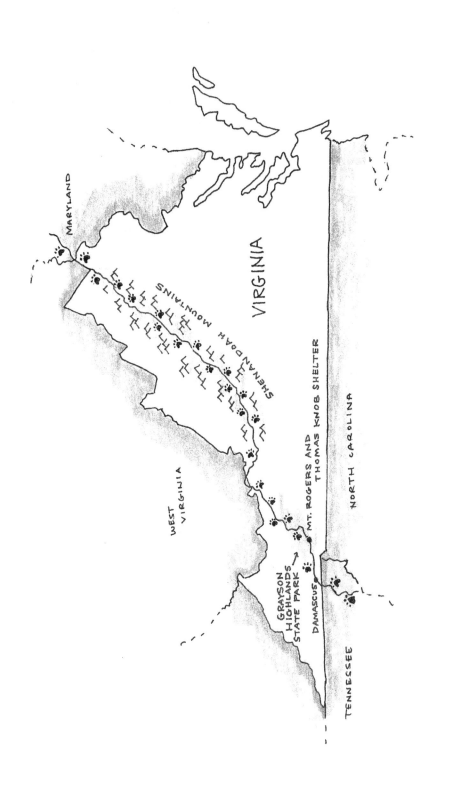

CHAPTER 7
Virginia Ventures

"It feels good to be hiking in the sunshine, doesn't it buddy? We just need to keep following the white blazes and we'll soon be in Virginia. These 15 mile hiking days will get us there in a flash."

It took another couple of weeks of hiking to get through the rest of the Tennessee section, but the weather got steadily warmer as we went. I could tell that spring was finally on its way. We met lots of friends along the way and played a game that I like. We pass our friends and then they pass us. We pass them again and then they pass us. It makes hiking fun because you never know who you will meet coming toward you and who you will see as they pass you. David always smiles and greets everyone, and of course, they all have to say hello to me. Sometimes I even get pats or rubs and sometimes ear scratches!

Finally, though, we were in the final stretch of trail that leads into Damascus, Virginia where David's mom and her friend, Renea, had driven up to visit us. David took a "zero day" to visit with them and eat his mom's good cooking. A zero day is a day in which a hiker hikes zero miles in order to relax and rest his body, just like I did when I was sick. I like zero days, and I like David's mom's cooking!

We got to Damascus early in the morning. David's mom and Renea were already waiting at the trailhead. Renea is a section hiker on the A.T., and she wanted to hike a short section with David. He gave big hugs to his mom and Renea, and they gave me some belly rubs, a few scratches behind the ears and a big hug as well. To reward them for their efforts, I gave them both a wet kiss on the nose.

"I'm looking forward to a nice hot shower, a comfy bed, and some good home cooking," said David. "Speaking of which, whatcha got in that cooler?"

"I've made all your favorites," said David's mom. "Barbecue ribs, corn, potato salad, coleslaw, baked beans, and carrot cake for dessert."

"*Ohhh…* you're killin' me!" moaned David. "This shower is gonna be quick! I am ready to EAT!"

She winked at me and said, "I also cooked up a little something for Copper: his very own special beef stew."

I liked the sound of that.

We ate well, slept well, and enjoyed our short visit that night. As the sun came up, David was up and packing his backpack and mine, filling them with yummy leftovers from dinner. Then, it was time to go.

"I'm going to miss you Copper dog!" said David's mom as she roughed up my fur and gave me my favorite ear scratches. "You take care of David, you hear me?"

I gave her a playful nuzzle, and then we were on our way. David and I were once again on the trail.

It was an uphill day and very tiring, but I was used to that. We enjoyed walking in the Virginia sunshine and chatting with other hikers as we passed them on the trail.

According to David, we had hiked over 300 miles. My legs and body had become much stronger since I left home, but I enjoyed my morning and afternoon breaks to take a nap and eat a snack.

We hiked about 10 miles that day, and as night began to fall, David said, "I'm having trouble finding a good place to set up the tent, Copper. We need to find one soon because it's going to start raining any minute now." We doubled our pace and kept looking for a good spot to camp. When the raindrops began to fall, David finally gave up.

"Well, Copper, there are no level surfaces out here. I guess we'll have to camp on the side of this hill. This should make for an interesting night of sleep."

He set up the tent, rushing to beat the rain, and arranged his sleeping bag the best he could. I was okay, but David just couldn't seem to get comfortable on the slope. Then, just as we'd gotten settled down for the night, it happened. Thunder! Lightning! Boom! Bang!

"It's okay, Copper. It's just a thunderstorm." said David as he pulled me closer to him and stroked my fur.

David doesn't understand why I am so deathly afraid of thunderstorms. He doesn't know how I lost my mother and my first family. I don't want to lose David, but I had to let him know that the storm was dangerous and potentially deadly.

David dozed off to the sound of thunder and pouring rain, but I stayed awake and worried. Water began to fill the floor of our tent, and I kept moving to get away from it. It was filling the floor, and soaking the sleeping bag. When I couldn't stand it anymore, I stood up and leaned over David, panting and pushing on the door flap.

"Oh, no!" said David, as he scrambled from his sleeping bag. He quickly opened the tent flap, and proceeded to sweep the water out of the tent.

"I knew setting the tent on this hillside was a bad idea but I had nowhere else to put it! The hill funneled the water straight into our tent!" He stepped out into the storm and started frantically digging a channel to divert the water.

As he dug the channel and desperately tried to get the water out of the tent, the storm raged on. Lightning was flashing all around us. I was sure that we were in danger, and I wanted a safe place to hide from the storm.

"Copper, stay right there. You're fine and we'll both get back in the tent as soon as I get it dry. Don't leave. The thunder and lightning won't hurt you."

I did as he said, but I knew better. I knew that lightning could hurt you and even kill you. My skin prickled, my fur standing on end. I shivered and panted uncontrollably. Thunder! Lightning! Boom! Bang! The lightning was striking all around us. It was so loud and bright! I started running as fast as I could to get away from the noise and the blinding light.

David yelled, "Copper, STOP! COME BACK HERE!"

But I was gone! I had to get away from my greatest fear. I ran and ran, finally ducking into a culvert under a highway to wait out the worst of the storm. As the terrible thunder and lightning raged on, I shivered in the darkness.

Finally, it was over and I began to return to my senses. I came out of the culvert and started making my way back to David. I knew he would be worried about me, but in my panicked flight, I hadn't paid attention to where I was going. I had no idea how to get back to where he was. He was just right up the hill, or so I thought. I tried sniffing the ground and sniffing the air, but the scents on the trail had been washed away by the torrential rain. I ran and ran turning this way and that, but I couldn't find David. Finally, exhausted, I curled up behind a rock and waited. What if I didn't find David? What if

David couldn't find me? What if there was no way for us to be reunited? Would David finish the trail without me and leave me behind? I didn't want to think about it anymore. I closed my eyes and tried to sleep as soft rain continued to fall.

When the sun came out the next morning, everything seemed better. Except for one thing. I still couldn't find David. I walked along the road hoping to see him, but instead I saw a man and a woman sitting in a car on the side of the road. As I approached the car, a friendly woman got out and walked toward me. I wagged my tail and put my head down to let them know I was friendly too.

"Hey, puppy," said the lady. "What are you doing out here all soaking wet? Where's your family?"

The man came around to see who she was talking to and said, "He must be lost. See this collar around his neck? It has a tag on it. It says his name is Copper, and he belongs to David. We need to call this phone number."

I was so thankful that David had gotten me a new collar and tag. The man from the car immediately called the number on my tag, but no one answered. He waited a few minutes and then tried again. Still no answer.

"We can't just leave him here. He's beautiful, but he's so wet and cold that he's shivering. Why don't we take him home, get him dry, and try the phone number again later?" asked the lady.

The man agreed. They toweled me off, put me in their car and drove me to their house. They made a bed of towels for me to sleep on in their garage, fed me, and kept calling the number on my collar. No one answered.

They called all day and into the night, and still no one answered. I spent that night in their garage. I couldn't help but wonder if once again, I would have to find a new family. I wondered if this was going to be my new family. They were very good to me, but I knew David would be looking for me. The nice man and woman left me a bowl of water, and told me that they were still trying to get in touch with David.

About mid-morning the next day, they tried calling one more time. David answered. I could hear his voice, and I immediately stood up, started wagging my tail, and put my ear to the phone. They found David!

The man said, "We've found your dog. He's safe and warm and dry."

I heard David say, "Thank goodness you found him. He ran away during the storm night before last, and I have been desperately looking for him. My cell phone battery was dead, and I had to find a way to get off the trail to get to a place to charge it. I finally found a place this morning right before I got your call."

The nice couple agreed on a place to meet David so that I could be returned to him. As we neared the meeting place, I saw him from the car and got very excited. When they opened the car door, I bounded out and ran straight into his open arms. He embraced me, then clipped a leash onto my collar.

"I can't thank you enough for taking care of him," David told the couple. "He's always been afraid of storms, but I didn't ever think I would lose him in one. You've been very kind. Thank you again."

"No problem." said the man. "He's a great dog and was no trouble at all."

"Bye, Copper!" said the woman as she knelt to give me a hug. "You be a good boy."

I thanked her with a quick, wet nose kiss.

As we hiked away, I was very glad to be back with my hiking buddy and friend. He didn't scold me at all, and I was glad for that.

He just said, "I missed you, buddy. We've got to work on your fear of those storms. You scared me, and I just couldn't hike on without you."

Little did we know that our luck with storms was about to get worse as we made our way to Mount Rogers on another wet, rainy, cold, and extremely windy night. The wind was ripping at our backpacks and pushing us as we walked. When we had tolerated the weather long enough to be exhausted, we stopped at Thomas Knob shelter. It was so windy that the hikers were afraid that the roof of the shelter was going to be blown off. The wind was blowing the rain sideways into the shelter and getting everybody and everything wet. The hikers tried to build a wall with a ground cover to keep the rain out. But the wind just whipped it loose each time they finished tying it off. It was quite a storm!

David looked for a place within a low, protected thicket to pitch his tent so that we could both be out of the storm, but there were rocks everywhere. The few suitable spots for tents were already occupied. Sleeping in the shelter was the only option for David.

I was on a leash and was lying under the picnic table when things got really bad. The picnic table provided no cover because of the sideways rain. I was getting hit pretty hard. David looked all around for a better place for me to sleep out of the fierce wind and rain. Finally, he found a huge rock under the shelter for me to lie behind. Then, he put down a water repellent ground cover over the mud, put his own sweater and rain jacket on me for warmth, and hoped that the big rock would serve as a windbreak.

I curled up behind the rock but I was still shivering. I tried to curl tighter into myself but nothing seemed to help. As the night went on, things got colder and the wind got worse. David got up several times during the night to try to tie the ground cover back down and to check on me. I was cold and wet and wishing for a dry place. As it turned out, I wasn't the only one who wished I had a dry place to sleep.

Sometime during the night, Mudmouth, a thru-hiker from Kentucky that had passed us earlier in the day, also woke up and came down to the rock to check on me. She couldn't stand seeing me shivering in the cold and rain and loudly exclaimed, "Enough is enough!"

She scooped me up in both arms and bodily hauled me up into the shelter, waking Ambo who was sleeping next to her and shouted, "Can Copper sleep here?" leaving me within inches of Ambo's sleeping bag.

"Yeah," Ambo answered, "That's fine."

"Thanks," yelled Mudmouth. "I am just so worried about him out there in the wind and rain, He's freezing to death."

David woke up at her shouting over the sound of the wind-blown tin roof, which was scratching and ripping at the nails that held it down. He saw what she had done and pulled me onto his mat and tucked me under his legs for warmth. I was out of the wind but still very cold and wet.

The next morning, Ambo announced that it had gotten down to 18 degrees Fahrenheit during the night. It was far too cold to stay warm in that blustery wind. I was very thankful that Mudmouth brought me into the shelter, and so was David. He thanked her for her thoughtfulness, but she dismissed it with a flick of her hand.

David stayed in his sleeping bag until the sun was high in the sky. I stayed right beside him to collect his warmth. After gathering our things and hoisting our packs into place, we began a nice walk through Grayson Highlands State Park while basking in the warmth of the sun.

Grayson Highlands was a fun place to hike because I got to meet new friends. There were so many small, wild ponies there! And, they were really friendly. We introduced ourselves by running and chasing each other and enjoying the sunshine. The ponies loved to run, and so did I.

David motioned me over under a tree and pulled our snacks from his pack. As we enjoyed our snack, the ponies came around and wanted to share our food. David didn't have any extra to spare, and he knew he wasn't supposed to feed them according to the park rules. Feeding the ponies would make them become dependent on humans and that's not a good thing. The ponies are wild and need to remain so. Evidently, people didn't always follow the rules. The ponies became very interested when food appeared. Even though it looked as though the ponies liked the hikers, it was really their interest in food that made them approach.

Hikers weren't very likely to share their food, though. I learned very early in our hike that the hikers only carry enough food for themselves. They have a lot of supplies to carry and try to determine exactly how little food they can get by with until they can reach another town to resupply. Rarely do they carry anything extra. It seems, though, that there is *one* exception...food for celebrations.

Two weeks after we came out of the Mt. Rogers area, David stopped in town to buy an entire cake in a plastic cake box. He wedged it in the top of his pack and hiked out of town. He was starting his own hiker tradition. Every time he completed another quarter of the trail, he would eat a fraction of a cake equal to the fraction of the trail he had hiked already. When we completed ¼ of our hike, he ate ¼ of the cake he had brought and gave the rest to nearby hikers. He gave me a little bite since I was hiking with him. What a fun tradition.

The Shenandoah Mountains in Virginia provided warm and beautiful days. It was the beginning of spring and everything was in full bloom. The bees were buzzing, the flowers were blooming, the trees were budding, and baby animals of all kinds were in the woods. We saw baby squirrels, baby chipmunks, baby rabbits and baby deer. The woods were alive with babies.

Mothers can be very protective of their babies, so we gave the animals plenty of space. We were being respectful of all the animals and watching from a distance as they nurtured their newborns.

One day, David and I heard a rustling of leaves, and we both turned to determine the source of the disturbance. David suddenly pulled back on my leash when he saw the cause 150 yards ahead of us.

"Well, look what we have here," David whispered. "A mama bear and her three baby cubs. Let's just sit here and let them eat in peace."

A bear! Krystin had warned David about bears. She said that we would get *eaten* by a bear on the trail. This was my first bear encounter, and I didn't know what to expect.

David put his hand on my collar and we both sat quietly on a fallen log and watched the mama and her babies at a distance as they ate berries in the sunshine.

Suddenly, the mama bear put her nose in the air, turned her body towards us and had her black eyes focused on me. She had located our scent and was on alert. The fur on my neck stood straight up, but I stood my ground and didn't flinch or blink. Within a flash, the mama bear turned on her heels and hustled her babies straight into the woods.

"Good boy, Copper. You did just right by staying still and quiet. We never want to startle a mama bear who has young cubs because they have strong instincts to protect their babies. They are very powerful animals and could kill you with one swipe of their powerful paws."

I can't wait to see Kristyn's face when David tells her that we saw four bears! He'll probably dream up some really good story about the bears in the Shenandoah Mountains who almost ate us alive and how we just barely made it out of the mountains in one piece. Then, David would give a hearty laugh and tell her the true story of the mama bear and her baby cubs happily eating berries in the sun, at which she'd probably just scowl and swat him on the arm for teasing her.

But it will be a long time before that could happen. We've been walking through Virginia for a month and a half already now, and we're *finally* about to reach a new state--and yet we aren't even close to being halfway done with the trail yet. It's been a gorgeous spring, if a bit wet for my liking, but it's already getting too hot to walk in the sun--and the hardest parts of the trail are yet to come.

Notes from the Appalachian Trail in Virginia

- I am very glad that I have a collar and a tag with my name, my family's name and phone number so that I can always find my way back to David.
- If I am to become a better trail dog, I need to become less afraid of thunder and lightning.
- A zero day is when a hiker takes a day of rest and hikes zero miles.
- Never bother a mama bear and her baby cubs. She will always do what it takes to protect her cubs.
- The Appalachian Trail through Virginia is about 552 miles.
- We have walked 840 miles and completed 38% of the Appalachian Trail.

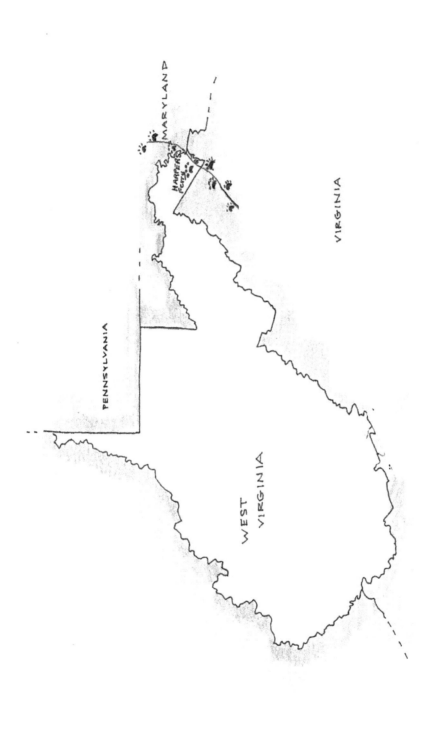

CHAPTER 8
West Virginia Wanderings

David and I had long anticipated reaching the town of Harpers Ferry, West Virginia, where the Appalachian Trail Conservancy headquarters is located. The hikers had been talking about Harpers Ferry for a few days and were very eager to get there. I ran ahead of David, because it sounded like something really important was ahead.

"Well, Copper, we are almost to the A.T. Conservancy and we are about to become a part of history."

I looked up at him with my big brown eyes and gave him my best "Whaaaaaat?" look.

He chuckled, rubbed my head, and said, "Each year, the Appalachian Trail Conservancy welcomes and records every Appalachian Trail hiker who visits them in Harpers Ferry. Each hiker gets a number that allows him or her to know how many hikers have already passed through on their way to the end of the trail. Hikers also get their picture made for the official A.T record books."

As we got to the building that had the Appalachian Trail symbol on it, a nice lady came outside and said, "Welcome to Harpers Ferry and the Appalachian Trail Conservancy. Come on in."

David said, "Thank you." and walked into the building after removing his pack.

Hey! What about me? I'm hiking this trail too! The lady turned and shut the door leaving me outside. I guess dogs don't count as hikers and can't get a picture made. It isn't fair.

I was so sad. Lying in the warm sun consoled me as I dreamed of what it must be like to be considered a *real* thru hiker.

Just as I was about to drift off to sleep, I heard the voice of the lady who let David in the door to the conservancy.

The nice lady smiled back at David and asked, "Is this the dog you were telling me about? Is this Copper?"

"The one and only," answered David.

"Is Copper hiking the rest of the way with you?"

"Yes," said David, "He's thru-hiking with me."

"Well, bring him inside!" she said. "All hikers are welcome in the hiker lounge, even hiker dogs!"

She gave David a big grin, gave me scratches behind both ears, and then moved aside to welcome us through the door and into the hiker lounge. She told us to make ourselves at home. David sat on the soft comfortable chairs, and I lay down on the soft, fluffy rug, wagging my tail in my joy at becoming an *official* hiker dog!

After we'd had a chance to rest, drink some water, and eat a snack, the nice lady asked us if we were ready to have our picture taken. David said that we were and we moved toward the door to have our picture made in front of the Appalachian Trail sign.

I stood proudly beside David as she snapped the photo. David put the picture into the trail record book, signed his real name and his trail name: *Blast*. Then he wrote *Copper* for me, and put a paw print as my signature. We were in the history books as official thru-hikers.

We visited with the nice lady for a little while longer, listening to her tales of the A.T. and what we were about to encounter. She wished us well, gave me a pat on the head, and said we were welcome to come back anytime.

And now, we're about to set off for the bridge out of West Virginia. The Appalachian Trail only goes through a small corner of West Virginia, so we'll be in and out in only one day. We're on our way to Maryland!

Notes from the Appalachian Trail in West Virginia

- I am called a thru-hiker even though I'm a dog.
- Hiker dogs are made to feel just as important as hiker humans at the A.T. Conservancy.
- Hikers who put their picture and name in the official A.T. log book become a part of history.
- Harpers Ferry is known as the emotional halfway point. For many hikers, it is the place where reality sets in that they have a good chance of finishing the trail even though they have only hiked about a third of the way.
- The Appalachian Trail through West Virginia is about 3 miles long.
- We have hiked 853 miles and completed 39% of the Appalachian Trail.

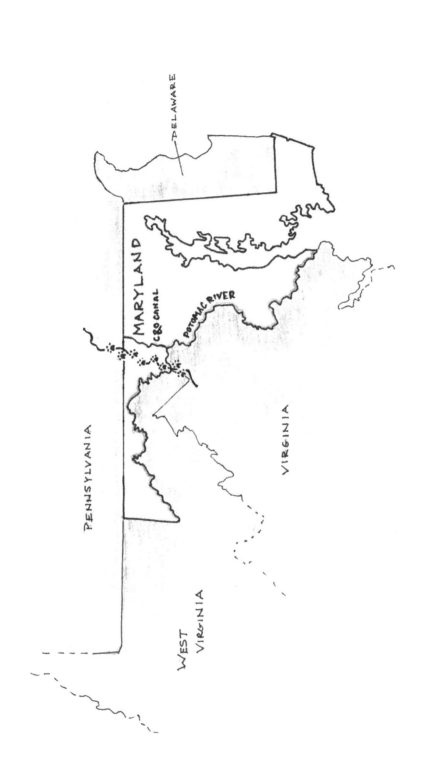

CHAPTER 9
Maryland and the Muskrat

Going into Maryland required the crossing of a bridge high over the Potomac River. I hate bridges. We've been over too many to count on this hike. I've had to cross rivers and streams both big and small across log bridges, wooden plank bridges, swinging rope bridges, and concrete bridges. The plank bridges and log bridges aren't too bad because they are usually low to the ground. The concrete bridges are easy because it is like walking on a road. The swinging rope bridge is terrifying. It is the worst so far. I was so scared crossing that bridge that my legs became paralyzed and I couldn't move. It was terrible. David had to physically shake me to snap me out of it and get me moving. He dragged me across, kicking and whining, by my collar. I don't ever want to do that again.

This was my first *metal* bridge. I could see the river running beneath my paws and could hear the rush of the water passing by. The bridge had big holes, the metal was scorching hot, and the stairs leading down to the water's edge were super steep. Each stair step had multiple holes and spiky things that cut into my paw pads. Through each hole, all I could see was water. Every fiber in my body was telling me this was dangerous. My inner voice was yelling, "Don't do it!"

I could tell that it was a long way down. David kept telling me to come on, but by this point, I was visibly shaking. Fear was racking my body and my feet refused to move. The stairs were straight down with no end in sight. It was happening again. Paralysis.

"Copper, let's go," yelled David.

I took a deep breath and put one paw onto the first step.

OUCH! Not only was it a long way down, but those spikes really hurt! I tried again with trembling legs and again my body screamed, NO!

David came up the stairs to look me in the eyes and said, "Copper, there's only one way to get down there and it is by these stairs. You've got to do this. I know it doesn't feel good on your paws but it won't actually hurt them. Please, just try."

I tried again, but I was terrified.

Another hiker came up as David was coaxing me down the stairs. He introduced himself as Boon.

"Can I help you get your dog down the stairs?" asked Boon. "It looks like he's having a little trouble."

"No thanks," replied David. "He doesn't like the stairs, but he needs to do this himself and conquer his fear."

"Alright," said Boon. "I'll see you down by the canal."

Seeing him fly past me on those stairs with no harmful results gave me a tiny boost of confidence. The stairs still hurt my paws but I kept moving down one step at a time. It took a long time on shaking legs and trembling paws, but I made it.

Fortunately, the end result was worth it all. David was proud of me and we were crossing another state line.

As we crossed into Maryland by way of the C&O canal towpath, I found water on both sides. That was a chance for me to slip into the water and cool off. David removed my pack and I jumped in. Ahhhh… it felt so good!

I walked in the water in the canal as David walked down the towpath beside the canal. We saw turtles lazing on rocks in the sun and a strange new creature in the water that I had never seen before.

Boon came up beside David and said, "Hey, did you see that animal in the water back there?"

"Yeah, I did," said David. "But, I only saw the head. Was it a beaver?"

"I don't think so," said Boon. "I think it is something different. Copper was sniffing at it and trying to get to it before it swam off. I don't think he was scared of it at all."

What was there to be scared of? Swimming critters can't poke your feet with metal spikes or suspend you 30 feet in the air over a rushing river!

We walked down to the water to determine what it was. I waded into the water to try to get close to it but had no luck.

"Look," David said as he got closer, "It's a muskrat! I've never seen one in real life, but I've seen them in lots of books. They are just large rodents that always live near the water. Can you see his tail? Muskrats have scaly looking tails with no fur on them. The cool thing is that their rear feet are webbed, just like a duck's, for swimming."

"I saw its feet!" said Boon excitedly. "You're right. They *are* webbed."

I kept trying to get in the water to play with him as we moved down the path, but he was a quick little thing and kept getting away. I finally gave up and came out of the water. David let me dry off a bit and then put my pack back on.

As we walked on, Boon said, "I wonder why this is called the C&O canal."

"It stands for the Chesapeake and Ohio Canal," David said. "It once was used for getting goods up and down the Potomac River. It sure makes for a pretty walk through Maryland, doesn't it?"

"That it does," answered Boon.

Soon, we turned away from the river and climbed up a steep cliff into the forests of Maryland. As dusk settled upon us, we began looking for a shelter or campsite in which to hang our hammock.

Since the Shenandoahs, we've been sleeping each night in a special kind of tent with a hammock inside. David had mailed his tent back home and asked his mom to send the hammock because it was lighter to carry and cooler to sleep in now that the weather has gotten so hot. There's a bug net that hangs over the hammock and falls all the way to the ground. The bug net has a zipper on the side and a floor on the bottom. Each night, David hangs the hammock between two trees, unzips the net, brings me inside, and zips it up behind us. I lie down on the flooring, while David climbs into the hammock above me. We sleep like that, one above the other, just like a portable bunk bed. There's also a rainfly that covers the hammock when we have to sleep in the rain. We can now sleep comfortably in heat, rain, or a cloud of bugs. No problem!

Now that summer had arrived, nights were muggy and days were very hot. David and I had a new habit. We would walk early in the morning, stop for lunch, sleep in the afternoon, and start walking again when the weather cooled off. I thought this was a great plan. It's what dogs do naturally when we travel. We don't like walking in the heat of the day, and neither does David.

Little did we know that this plan would be much needed in the heat of the states that we still had yet to hike through. The heat was beginning to take its toll on both of us and the ticks were clinging to us like glue.

Thankfully, after conquering my fear and crossing the metal bridge into Maryland, the days in this state were fairly uneventful. We only had to hike four days and 41 miles before we were completely out of the state and heading into Pennsylvania.

Notes from the Appalachian Trail in Maryland

- Muskrats are actually rodents who live near water and have webbed back feet for swimming.
- Walking on the trail is *much* less stressful than crossing over water on metal steps with holes in them!
- The C&O canal was actually used in the 1800's and early 1900's to take goods up and down the Potomac River. Now it is a historical site and no longer used.
- Sleeping in a bug net sure is nice at night when the bugs come out and start to swarm.
- The Appalachian Trail through Maryland is about 41 miles.
- We have hiked 894 miles and completed 41% of the Appalachian Trail.

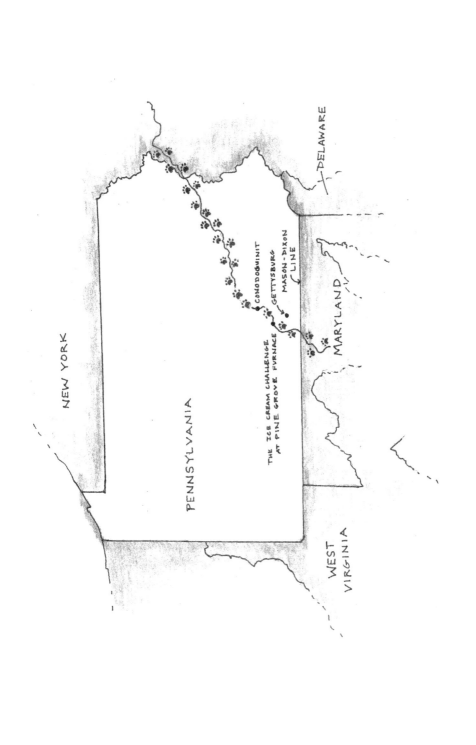

NEW YORK

PENNSYLVANIA

THE ICE CREAM CHALLENGE
AT PINE GROVE FURNACE

CONODOGWINIT

GETTYSBURG

MASON-DIXON
LINE

DELAWARE

MARYLAND

WEST
VIRGINIA

CHAPTER 10
Pennsylvania Perseverance

"There's the sign, Boon!" yelled David. "We've officially crossed from Maryland into Pennsylvania."

"I've heard about this line my whole life," said Boon. "The Mason-Dixon Line. My mom is from Pennsylvania and my dad is from Maryland. They were always teasing each other about being above or below the Mason-Dixon Line."

"I learned about it in history class." said David. "During the Civil War in the 1800's, it became a symbolic line between the slave states and the free states. Lots of blood was shed on the battlefields of Gettysburg right here in Pennsylvania as the north fought the south. Two surveyors, Charles Mason and Jeremiah Dixon, established the boundary back in the mid 1700's after surveying the land. They placed rocks right here to formally establish the border between the two states."

"Let's take a picture of each other in front of the sign," said Boon. "I know my parents will want to see this!"

"Come on, Copper," said David, motioning me toward the sign. "Let's strike a pose for Boon to remember us by."

Boon snapped the picture, and laughed. "A picture of a handsome gentleman and a hairy animal for my collection."

He came over to give me some ear scratches and said, smirking, "You know you're the gentleman, right, Copper? I'll see you guys down the trail. Take care of Blast, won't ya?" And with that, he hiked on.

It was hot in Pennsylvania in late June and we had been hiking in the heat for several days. We were sweating buckets, and so was everyone else we passed along the way. The trail was flat and open with hardly a shade tree to be found. Trudging in the heat made me long for water. We passed by a working farm with lots of cows and entered into the woods surrounding Conodoguinit Creek. The water looked so inviting.

I looked longingly at the creek and then looked up at David. Just as I looked back toward the creek, David said, "C'mon, Copper, let's go swimming."

David took off my pack, pulled off his clothes down to his boxer shorts, and took off running. I was right behind him. I couldn't wait to swim in that cool water.

Just as we hit the water, David plunged himself under, came up laughing out loud, and said, "Well, well, what do we have here but the Conodoguinit with a Copper dog in it!"

Sometimes he cracks himself up with his own strange brand of humor.

We had much fun swimming and lying in the warm sun. We splashed and played until the sun began to set in the sky and it was time to go.

After toweling off with David's camp towel, we put our packs back on and headed down the trail. As we walked, David said, "All that swimming made me hungry, Copper".

So what's new?, I thought. Hikers are always thinking about food because they are always hungry. They need lots of calories to have enough energy to hike the trail. Many of the A.T. traditions focus on food. One of those traditions is called the Half-Gallon Challenge.

The Half-Gallon challenge takes place at the Pine Grove Furnace General Store. As we topped the hill on our way there, we were surprised to see that Cricket, Trixie, and Roscoe had already arrived.

"Blast! Copper! We haven't seen you in a while," yelled Cricket.

"That could be because this miserable heat has slowed you down enough to let us catch up with you," said David. "If you'd just start hiking early and go swimming as soon as it gets hot like us, you wouldn't have to stop so often! Or are you just intentionally stalling to put off getting into the rocky part of the state?"

"You caught us," said Cricket. "We are not at all looking forward to the rest of this state. But you *are* going to like this small section of Pennsylvania because you are about to experience the treat of your life," said Cricket. "A half-gallon of ice cream to celebrate making it half way to Maine. The official Half-Gallon Challenge is about to commence."

"Sounds great," said David. He went in the store and came out a few minutes later with a tub of chocolate peanut butter ice cream.

He sat down on a bench and dug a wooden spoon into the cold, sweet treat. His face dissolved into an expression of bliss as the spoon slid down his tongue, and he tore into the ice cream with wild abandon. As he was finishing his treat, another hiker topped the hill and David invited her to join them.

"Come on over and join us in a brain freeze. This ice cream tastes wonderful, and having something cold to eat is exceptional in this heat. It has taken me all of 21 minutes to eat this half gallon of ice cream."

"Sounds perfect," said the newcomer. "I already know which ice cream I'm choosing."

"Which?"

"Rocky road! To prepare me for the miles of pointy rocks that Pennsylvania has in store for me."

"How appropriate!" said David, laughing. "I'd bet Rocky Road was invented by a Pennsylvania A.T. hiker! By the way, I'm Blast, and that's Copper, my dog; Cricket; her dog, Roscoe; and her sister Trixie."

"Good to finally see you all in person instead of just reading about you in the logs," the newcomer said. "I'm Pickles. I've been behind you folks for a while, but I practically ran here to get me some of that ice cream. I will join you all in two shakes." She dropped her pack, and slipped inside the store to get her own half gallon, and came out a moment later to take a seat on the rail and dig into her cold treat.

While David and Pickles were chatting, Trixie sat her almost empty ice cream carton on the porch rail and grabbed her head, saying, "Brain freeze...ugggghh....it hurts!"

Trixie lay her head down on the grass and rolled from side to side moaning and holding her head. I looked from her to her ice cream and then looked at her again. Should I? She wasn't looking and I couldn't resist it any longer. I had watched everyone enjoying ice cream and no one had offered me a single bite. I slipped past Trixie and knocked her ice cream from the rail. She didn't budge and no one else noticed. I made a tentative step toward the ice cream carton and still no movement from Trixie. That was my signal...the ice cream was mine! I snatched the carton up with my teeth and ran to the corner to enjoy what little bit was left of Trixie's tasty treat. Now I knew what all the fuss was about. This stuff was good!

Just as I had polished off the rest of the carton, Trixie raised up, looked at the railing, and said, "Hey, what happened to the rest of my ice cream?"

"Ahem, look in the corner at the furry one," answered Pickles, pointing at the empty carton.

"You little thief," said Trixie. "I guess you wanted to participate in the Half-Gallon Challenge too, huh bud?"

"Here, Trixie, let me buy you another half-gallon," said David. "Which kind would you like?"

"No, thanks," said Trixie. "He actually did me a favor because I've still got terrible brain freeze from what I've already eaten."

Whew! That was close. Thank goodness she wasn't mad.

They visited for a while longer and David decided that we needed to move on.

"Hey, Pickles, Cricket, Trixie, we're going to visit Gettysburg tomorrow if all of you want to come with us."

"Sure, we'd love to," answered Pickles. "Right, Cricket?"

"Sounds good to me," said Cricket.

It was noon when our shuttle arrived in Gettysburg the next day, and it was sweltering hot in the midday sun. Roscoe and I were scanning the landscape for the perfect shade tree.

Pickles interrupted my search for shade and asked the group: "You want to know something interesting about Lincoln and his Gettysburg address?"

"Let's hear it," answered David.

"Lincoln's Gettysburg Address came after a three hour speech by the governor. Can you imagine listening to a speech that long and knowing that there was another speech about to be given? Well, when Lincoln gave his speech, the audience was totally silent. Lincoln took their silence as disappointment in his words. They weren't disappointed; they were stunned. It was such a powerful speech that even today almost anyone can recite at least the beginning of the Gettysburg Address if not the whole thing."

"A little history lesson from Pickles," quipped Trixie.

"At your service," laughed Pickles. "Just trying to educate my fellow hikers as I tumble through the rocks of Pennsylvania."

We spent the rest of the day at Gettysburg walking the battlefield. I was enjoying being with Pickles and Roscoe, but I was tired and hot. I just wanted to go back to the campsite where I could find sweet relief from the heat. Or so I thought.

We caught a shuttle back to our campsite around dusk, but I found little relief there. The night was hot, muggy, and buggy. We managed to get only a little sleep before continuing on into the Cumberland Valley the next day. When would the heat wave dissipate?

As we walked, we both tried to ignore how miserable we were. It was already sweltering just an hour after sunrise. I was lost in my daydream about a nice cool lake appearing just around the bend, but no such refreshment was in sight.

All of a sudden, I heard David moan and say, "Ummmmm, so good!" Then I saw him off in the bushes in the tall grass. He was picking blackberries and popping them in his mouth. As quick as he picked one, he was tossing it in his mouth with one hand while his other hand found another. I'd never seen anyone pick and eat blackberries as fast as he did. He offered one for me to taste, but I declined. Blackberries don't smell like anything that I would enjoy. A shade tree...or a nice, cool pond...now that's what I would enjoy!

Walking through the tall grass in Pennsylvania led to nightly tick removals. There were ticks on David's pants and shirts and ticks in my fur. Every night in the shelter we did a tick check, during which David removed the ticks from himself and me. At one point, he pulled thirty ticks from my fur, and that was after just one day in the woods.

Due to the intense heat, we were waking up early and getting on the trail at first light. Hiking in the early part of the day brought relief from scorching rays of the sun. Pennsylvania is not only hot, but as

Pickles said back at the general store, it has lots of rocks: big rocks, pointed rocks, tiny pebbles, and boulders.

It didn't help much that the rocks were very slippery from all the rain the past few days. As we were crossing the rocks, David and I both slipped and fell numerous times. David had one pretty nasty fall right in the middle of a boulder field.

No one could have prevented the fall, but, thankfully, David was fine. David looked up at me and said, "Well, I guess that's just one of many falls that I can expect as we maneuver through the tippy-topply rocks of Pennsylvania."

We continued our hike through Pennsylvania, and somehow scrambled over all the scorching rocks without any more spills. The pads on my paws were really getting sore from the jagged edges of the rocks and the blistering heat. Every chance I got, I found a soft spot of ground and stood perfectly still to allow my paws some relief. I'd been through some tough times in my life, but I had never encountered such pain on my paws. The heat felt as though it were searing my skin. Licking them did nothing to stop the pain and there was nowhere to lay my weary body. When the rocks were at their worst, I fell further and further behind David. Eventually, he looked back, saw how far behind I was, and came back through the rock field to check on me.

He saw me licking my paws and said, "It looks like these rocks are wreaking havoc on your feet. Your paws aren't used to these hot, sharp surfaces."

He opened my backpack and reached in for the paw protectant salve that he had brought just for this purpose. David pulled me onto his lap and then very carefully rubbed the waxy salve onto each pad of my paw. He was very careful to make sure that he put enough to soothe and protect them as much as possible.

As he finished with the salve, he took out the snow boots and put them on as a second means of protection and asked, "How's that buddy? Any better?"

I nudged his hand with my nose and gave him a kiss. It definitely was better but still hurting.

"Come on, boy. We only have a little way to go to get to the shelter and get off of these rocks. I've got a treat and can't wait to enjoy it! Of course, you'll get one too."

We made our way past the shelter and chose a spot to hang our hammock. Then we headed back to the shelter, where we made some new friends: Lady, Abe, and Two Ducks were relaxing there, and I introduced myself to them with kisses. David shook hands with them all around, then took a seat in the shelter.

"Look what I brought," said David, as he pulled a slightly smushed cake from the top of his backpack.

"Yum!" cried Lady. "I just know that's all for me!"

"Well, not all of it." said David. "Since I started hiking in North Carolina, I am now at *my* halfway point. I've decided to eat half of a cake to celebrate. I ate a fourth of a cake back in Virginia. I'll get to eat a whole cake when I finally climb Springer Mountain back in Georgia."

"Aha," said Lady. "That means I get the other half, right?"

David laughed and said, "Of course, but you should share it with Two Ducks and Abe as well, don't you think?"

"Yeah, Lady" said Abe and Two Ducks, "We did catch you when you almost fell on those rocks back there," they teased.

"You guys know I'm going to share it with you. After all, a *Lady* always shares what she has. And, I'm gonna give Copper just a little piece too. Come on over here and dig in!" laughed Lady as she took a giant bite from the already sad-looking smushed cake. She gave me a little bite, and said, "Let's celebrate heading into New Jersey soon."

I'll eat to that!

NORTHBOUNDERS
Notes from the Appalachian Trail in Pennsylvania

- Hikers think about food all the time. Those funny little traditions of eating cake and ice cream at celebration points are fun to watch.
- There's a lot of history to be learned along the trail.
- The trail often provides exactly what you need: food growing wild, and great swimming holes for cooling off.
- Other times, all it gives you is a lot of pesky little ticks.
- The Appalachian Trail through Pennsylvania is about 230 miles.
- We've traveled 1,124 miles and have completed 51% of the Appalachian Trail.

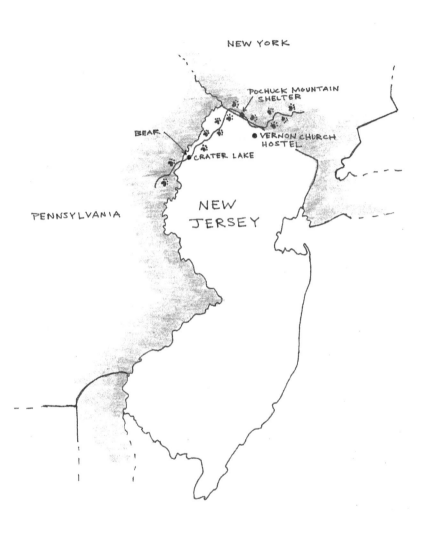

CHAPTER 11
New Jersey Naughtiness

After braving the rocks in Pennsylvania, we were very happy to cross the border into New Jersey. We were hoping for easier hiking conditions and better weather, but what we got was thousands and thousands of bugs!

They flew in and out of my ears, buzzed around my eyes, and flew all around my nose. David tried using some insect repellent which did absolutely no good. To survive the swarms, he resorted to his head net. It's a strange looking thing. It goes on like a hat but has a net that covers his face and ties around his neck. The net has little holes in it for breathing, but they are too small to let the bugs in. What a great invention. Sure do wish they made them for dogs!

David was much happier with the bug net over his head, and I was just happy to be walking to try to get away from the bugs. Just over the border into New Jersey, we passed Crater Lake and I wanted so badly to jump in. It was as if David read my mind.

"I know you want to go swimming, buddy, and so do I," said David, "but swimming is forbidden in Crater Lake."

I was disappointed, but kept hiking. We climbed straight up a rock wall to the cliff that ran along the lake. At least it was nice to be near the water. David sat down on a rock, pulled a bagel from his pack, and gave me a dog treat. While I was eating, I lifted my snout as I detected a familiar smell. Then, we heard a snapping, clomping, and crunching sound. David and I turned around just in time to spot a young black bear galloping speedily down the hill through the underbrush. David had told me that we would see a bear in New Jersey, but we didn't expect to see one so quickly. There's another bear story for Kristyn!

While walking along the New Jersey/New York border headed for the Pochuck Mountain Shelter, we made a couple of new hiker friends. They had had a tough day of hiking and came up beside David to chat.

"That sure is a beautiful dog you have there."

"Thanks. His name is Copper and I'm Blast," said David.

"I'm Bottlecap and this is Magic Scout"

"I have to ask," said David. "What's the story on your names?"

"Well mine is a little embarrassing," answered Bottlecap. "I was the brilliant soul who bought a six pack of Cokes in bottles from a little store in the town of Damascus. I brought them back to the hostel to share and forgot to bring a bottle opener. The hostel owner didn't have one so I spent about 30 minutes wrestling with all six bottles trying to get the caps off. What was supposed to be a nice gesture toward my fellow hikers turned into bloody fingers for me! I can laugh about it now, but I was pretty irritated with myself at the time."

"And I," said Magic Scout, "am just what my name implies. I have a unique sense of direction and can find anything, anywhere, anytime. Just let me scout out the area and like magic, I can find whatever it is that needs finding. I know it sounds weird but my parents tell me that I've been this way since I was a toddler."

"Sounds like a good skill," chuckled David. "Are you both stopping at the next shelter for the night?"

"We sure are. It's been a tough day."

"What happened to make it so tough?" asked David.

"Nothing that every other hiker doesn't have to go through," replied Bottlecap. "I just think that we are both so tired that every little hill seems like a mountain and every rock seems like a boulder. We just need some rest and we'll be fine tomorrow. We're running on empty right now."

As they continued chatting, I thought that I heard something in the woods. Leaves were rustling and there was an unfamiliar smell in the air. Something small was moving through the grass. A small, tasty critter. Dinner! Just then, I saw it in the dark and took out after it.

I raced through the woods in the darkness after a blur in the distance. It looked like a squirrel. Squirrels make a tasty meal, and I was going to catch this one. There he was, just behind the rock. I could taste the goodness already. Then just as I was about to pounce, this creature lifted its big fluffy tail and sprayed something in my face. OUCH! It stung my eyes terribly. Rubbing my face back and forth in the grass, I tried desperately to get the stinging stuff out of my eyes and off of my face. Not only did it sting, but it stunk! A squirrel had never done that to me before! Then I saw that it wasn't the same color as a squirrel: it was black with a white stripe down the back. I'd heard of these!

"Ewwwwww!" cried Bottlecap. "What is that disgusting smell?"

"Gross! Yuck! That stinks!" exclaimed Magic Scout. "I'm outta here!"

And they practically ran off without another word, noses pinched between their fingers.

We walked for another four miles with that stinky smell until we finally got to the shelter where we planned to camp. David tied me up far away from the shelter, and then went to join Bottlecap and Magic Scout as they ate their dinner.

"What was that awful smell back there?" asked Bottlecap.

"Copper got into a skunk," answered David.

Aha! That's what it was!

"What are you going to do about that smell?" asked Bottlecap.

"There is nothing I can do tonight except leave him downwind and sort it out tomorrow."

I was listening to their conversation as I waited down by the tree. It was obvious that my antics did not make me any new friends. I smelled awful! To try to clean myself, I kept rolling in the grass. It was no use. The smell of skunk just wouldn't go away.

The worst part of all of this is that nobody wanted to be near me. The hikers were having a good laugh up in the shelter, and I was downwind with the awful smell and the pesky bugs! I didn't even get to sleep in the bug net of the hammock that night because I smelled so bad. I sure hoped David could fix the mess I'd gotten myself into.

After a fitful night's sleep, morning finally arrived. David brought my breakfast to me and said, "Sorry buddy, but you've got to eat by yourself. You smell too bad to be around anybody this morning. We'll go into town and try to find a solution."

David and I walked all alone for quite a while until we found the side road that would lead towards town. I was walking as fast as I could because I just wanted to be there and get this stinky smell off.

We *finally* made it into town. David was very careful to put me under a tree downwind from the local store to try to find some help for our problem. Thank goodness the smell wasn't on *him*. David wouldn't even pet me for fear he would smell just as bad. Just as he got to the corner of the store, the owner came around the building carrying a sack of groceries. I heard her say, "Can I help you with something? Whew! I think I know what you need help with. That is NOT a good smell."

David replied, "Yes, ma'am, I hope you can help. My dog had a wrestling match with a skunk last night and he smells really bad. We're hiking the A.T. and he has a backpack on that smells equally as bad. Can you tell me what to do?"

"It happens to the best of us around here," said the lady, laughing. "Sure, I can help."

"The hikers back at the campsite told me to wash everything including my dog with tomato juice. Is that the best thing to do?" asked David.

"Well, I've heard that too, but it's never worked for me. Fortunately, I've found a perfect solution that works every time. My own sons had a few skunk sprays in their youth. I always tried to tell them not to mess with a skunk, but they were stubborn and had their fun. That stink is the skunk's defense. The oily substance he sprays when he's frightened not only smells bad but also gets in your eyes and all over your body. It can make a grown man cry. I'll bet your dog's eyes were watering pretty badly."

The lady looked at me and just laughed. "You look pitiful," she said as she looked down at me, "but we'll fix you right up."

"You'll need hydrogen peroxide, baking soda, and dish detergent. The hydrogen peroxide and baking soda will neutralize the odor and the dish detergent will help to get that oily substance off. It may take a few washes of the backpack and the dog, but it will work."

"Thanks," said David. "Where can I go to wash them both?"

"You are welcome to that old washtub and the garden hose out back behind the store. That old wash tub has had its share of skunk smells in it. Come on, let's get your supplies."

David bought what we needed and then we went behind the store to the hose and wash tub. He spent a long time washing me and my backpack. He had a system. Wash. Rinse. Repeat. Wash. Rinse. Repeat. After *many* washings, I finally started to feel clean and smelled so much better. Before we left to thank the lady for the use of her tub and water, David once again had to remove those pesky ticks that seem to live in my fur and skin. This time he removed 25 ticks. I guess ticks don't mind a skunk smell!

"Ok, buddy. It looks like we've got this problem whipped," said David.

I looked at him with my most *I'm really sorry* look.

"I know you were hunting," said David. "But, no more skunks, okay?"

I wish I could tell him that I will never ever, never ever, never ever, come near a skunk again. Lesson learned!

Notes from the Appalachian Trail in New Jersey

- Never mess with skunks!
- Hydrogen Peroxide, baking soda, and dish detergent will remove skunk smells from dogs, clothes, and backpacks.
- New Jersey has many bears and ticks.
- Wearing a bug net is imperative during the height of bug season!
- The Appalachian Trail through New Jersey is 72 miles.
- We have walked 1196 miles and completed 54% of the Appalachian Trail.

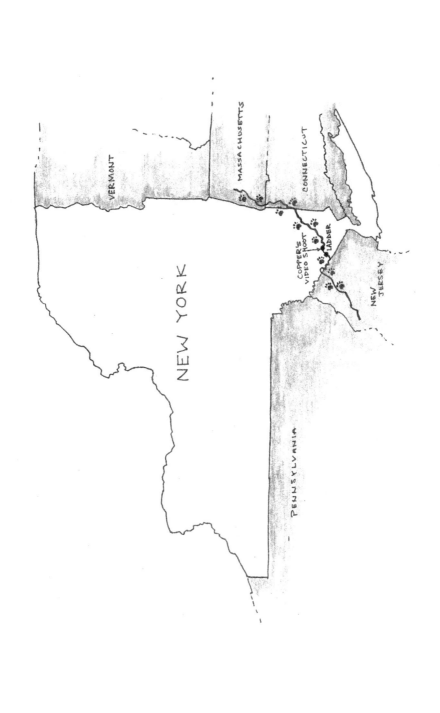

CHAPTER 12
New York Nosedive

All was well as we walked into New York except for one small irritation. It was so hot! Even hotter than Pennsylvania. It seemed like it was the hottest I had ever felt in my entire life. The good news, however, is that New York had *lots* of ponds for us to swim in.

It took us a long time to get through New York because we spent our days swimming and our late afternoons and early evenings walking. Some of the hikers kept moving slowly forward down the trail even during the hottest part of the day. As they passed us, we could tell that they were miserable from the unstoppable heat wave.

New York gave us some challenging and scary moments as we hiked through the state. At one point, the trail ran right into the sheer vertical side of a boulder and continued on top of it. The only way to follow the trail was up the ladder that had been secured to the boulder with steel cable. I had no idea how I was going to get over that boulder or up that ladder.

"Ok, Copper, we have another obstacle in our way and there's no way to get around it, so listen to me and do what I say. I'm going to put you on the ladder in front of me, place your feet on the rungs of the ladder and use my body to push you up. Then, I'll move your feet up one by one until we are at the top and over the boulder."

Putting my paws on that ladder brought back memories of that terrifying staircase over the Potomac River back in Maryland, and I steeled myself by remembering how well it had turned out. I called on that same inner strength now to help me quiet the fear. I knew that I had to dig down deep and trust David to get me over this boulder. But that didn't mean I had to like it.

"That's it, buddy. Just one step at a time."

My legs started trembling and fear gripped me as he moved each paw up. There was nothing but rocks below us and boulders above us. Things were moving too slowly. There was no way I was going to make it over this boulder. I decided to use my body to help him.

As I placed one foot on the rung of the ladder, I gave a mighty push against David with my hind legs to propel myself upward. Just as my back feet were about to grasp the rung on the ladder, I felt myself flying backward through the air. I heard David let out a horrible sound as he landed on the rock below while holding tight to my belly.

I quickly scrambled to my feet to be sure that he was okay. I couldn't tell. He wasn't moving and his arms were limp.

I nuzzled him gently on the side of his head. *Come on David, talk to me! Tell me you're okay!* Still, he didn't move or speak. Was he dead? Had I killed my best friend with my stupid fear of heights and my overeagerness to help?

David had taken the brunt of the fall as he cradled me in his arms. I wasn't hurt at all. He had protected me with his own body. I waited and waited, gently nudging him and willing him to please wake up.

After what seemed like forever, David opened his eyes, groaned softly, and looked at me with those big blue eyes. He was alive! I touched my paw to his chest and he gently lifted his head. Moving slowly, he unbuckled his pack, removed the shoulder straps, lifted his chest, his arms, and then very slowly rose to his feet.

"That one stung a little," said David after he stood up. "We were lucky, buddy. That tumble could have seriously injured us both. Falling on that giant backpack saved our hides. I just got the wind knocked out of me. I'll be fine."

Those were the sweetest words I'd heard in quite a while. I knew the fall was my fault, but he wasn't even blaming me.

After a few minutes rest, while David composed himself, we started moving back towards the ladder.

"Ok, Copper, let's try this again, this time without the backpack. Just put one foot on the ladder, press against me, and then move your feet up. Go slow and steady. No pushing this time. There's no rush."

I did as he instructed and we finally got to the top. David pushed me up and over until I was standing on top of the boulder where I waited for him to go down the ladder to retrieve his pack. I wagged my tail to say thanks and waited as he climbed quickly up the ladder again.

As we walked toward the trees, two hikers came up behind us and one of them said, "Is that Blast and Copper? We were hoping to catch up to you two."

"I'm Little Engine and this is my husband and hiking partner, Timber. It's nice to finally meet you, Blast. I've been keeping up with you by reading the shelter logs. It seemed that we were always just a little bit behind you."

"Those shelter logs are quite handy, aren't they? I've been keeping up with a few hikers myself through those logs."

"Lots of hikers have told us that you were hiking the trail with a 10 year old dog. That's impressive. I can't believe he made it over that boulder back there. I want Copper to be in my video about the people on the Appalachian Trail. Is that okay with you, Blast?"

"Well, how about that, Copper?" laughed David. "You are going to be a movie star. Copper the hiking dog and million dollar movie star!"

Little Engine laughed out loud and said, "I don't know about the million dollar part, but I am hoping for a million views of my video!"

We took our position on the trail and Little Engine started the interview.

"So, Copper, what do you like most about being on the trail?"

I walked over to David and put my paw on his leg and looked up into his face.

"Well, I'll take that as you like being with Blast on the trail, Copper. Can you shake my hand?" asked Little Engine.

Of course I could. I gave her my paw and she said, "Folks, I have just shaken the paw of a bona fide Appalachian Trail thru-hiking dog."

"Blast, is it true that Copper is ten years old? Isn't that too old to be hiking the trail?" asked Timber.

"He's probably at least that age, but you'll have to ask him about being too old," answered David. "I let him tell me his abilities through his actions on the trail. Go ahead, ask him."

"Copper, don't you think you're a little too old to be hiking the Appalachian Trail?"

I certainly do not! I gave my best burst of energy down the trail, stopped on a dime, turned around, ran back toward the camera, stopped on a dime again, and leapt into the air. I finished with a few spins in the middle of the trail. *There, does that look like I'm too old?*

Timber laughed. "Ok, I guess you showed us."

Little Engine turned back towards David and said, "It's been nice meeting you Blast, and it was definitely a pleasure meeting Copper. That's a fine dog you have there."

As Little Engine leaned down to give me a hug, I gave her a kiss on her nose and raised my paw for a handshake.

"Hey, no fair!" said Timber. "I want a kiss too." I gave him my paw for a handshake, and as he leaned down to take it, I gave him my best kiss on his nose.

Little Engine continued to video us as we hiked on down the trail through New York to reach our next lake before it got too hot.

Before we were out of sight, she yelled, "I hope he makes it all the way to Maine."

Neither Little Engine nor David knew it, but I was hoping the very same thing.

Notes from the Appalachian Trail in New York

- There's always a way to get over a mountain when you have a good friend.
- Swimming is my favorite way to stay cool on hot summer days and there's no shortage of ponds here!
- I'm in my first movie in New York!
- We have walked 1,286 miles and completed 58% of the Appalachian Trail.

MASSACHUSETTS

RHODE ISLAND

CONNECTICUT

NEW YORK

BEAR MOUNTAIN

BRASSIE BROOK SHELTER

SHARON

BEARDED WOODS HOTEL

KENT • TORRINGTON

CHAPTER 13
Connecticut Chaos

Entering Connecticut from New York, we continued to have hot weather. There wasn't a heat wave, but it was still steamy. Mosquitos continued to swarm and ticks continued to thrive in my fur. I wasn't feeling like my usual self as we walked into Connecticut, but I didn't know why. I just felt tired. I couldn't figure out if it was the heat or the long walking days or just the fact that I was getting older by the day.

As we got to Kent, Connecticut, David wanted to visit the local library to put some audiobooks on his mp3 player to listen to on the trail. That meant that I got to rest.

I lay in the shade of a tree by the library for most of the morning and rested while David got some books. A few minutes later, the librarian came out to meet me and brought some treats and water.

"Hi there, Copper," she said as she rubbed my head. "I hear you are a pretty good hiking buddy."

David came out to check on me and overheard her comment. He nodded his head in agreement and said, "Yes, he is the absolute perfect hiking buddy. He's always ready to go when I am, he doesn't require much food, and he never talks too much."

The librarian laughed and said, "I guess that is a good point. You don't have to worry about him nagging or fussing or interrupting your thoughts." She gave me one more pat on the head and said, "Enjoy your shade tree, Copper. We've got some more work to do in the library."

She was really sweet, and I appreciated the treats and water, but I just wasn't feeling so good. She left them beside me, and I eventually nibbled on a treat and drank all of the water.

After David finished in the library, he came back out to get me and again checked me for ticks before we headed off to the shelter for the night.

"These ticks seem to love you, Copper," said David as he worked his hands through my fur. "That flea and tick medicine that I'm giving you just doesn't seem to be working. I just pulled 28 more ticks off of your body. I think I'll call Dr. Amy tomorrow and see if she has a solution."

As we started our climb back into the woods, I noticed that my joints were aching, and I still felt tired after resting all day. Soon, we were back to the shelter. David found a great place to hang his hammock and I bedded down in the bug net for a good night's rest. It felt good to have the cool night's breeze flowing through the net and be free from bugs and mosquitoes buzzing around my face. I quickly dozed off to sleep.

At first light, David was up and filling my breakfast bowl. Usually, I am eager to start crunching on those tasty bits of food. This morning, I had no interest. I could barely stand up. Eating seemed like a chore. David encouraged me to eat, and because I wanted to please him, I slowly ate most of it.

David was very concerned about me and it showed on his face. "Are you all worn out from walking, buddy? You just don't seem like you are having fun anymore."

All I wanted to do was to find a nice soft bed of leaves, curl up, and sleep, but I couldn't let David know that. I *had* to keep hiking… I *needed* to keep hiking… I *wanted* to be with David. I could do this! I kept thinking that all I had to do was put one foot in front of the other and keep moving. I had to be strong!

David loaded up the gear and put our pack on our backs. Then, we started down the trail. Thankfully, we started out slowly and it gave my joints time to warm up and move better. I wanted to walk, but every step I took seemed to be more painful than the last.

We covered big miles for the next few days and each morning when I awoke, I hoped that the walking would be easier, and I would be back to my old self. Unfortunately, each day, I felt worse. My entire body was a constant ache and my joints had never hurt so badly. I desperately tried to keep up and not let David know that my joints were screaming with pain with every step I took. Even vigorous petting hurt and I had always loved roughhousing with David.

My strength was waning day by day and now it seemed hour by hour. I wouldn't be able to continue at this pace without figuring out what was happening to my body. But, I was also scared of being left behind. Little by little, I began to slow my pace to indicate to David that I just couldn't go on. He begrudgingly slowed his hiking rhythm a bit and said, "You sure have been a slow poke lately. What's going on with you?"

I lay down on the side of the trail, lay my chin on his hiking boots, and pressed my nose towards the ground. I was ashamed and embarrassed.

David squatted next to me, put his fingers on the first joint on my leg and pressed. I let out a yelp and snapped at him to stop hurting me.

"It's okay boy, I'm just trying to find out what's going on with you. I'm not trying to hurt you."

I lay my head back in the dirt, and David pulled my arthritis medicine from the pack.

"Here, this should help until we can get to a place to rest. Bearded Woods Hostel is a couple of days hiking away. Maybe we can stay there for a few days until you are better."

On the night before we were to arrive at the hostel, I started feeling even worse. As a matter of fact, I couldn't even stand up by myself. I slept fitfully that night and when I awoke the next morning, David had to help me stand up. He held me in place, and then let me slowly start taking a few steps. My joints were hurting so badly, that every step I took felt like a knife was being jabbed into my legs. I felt achy all over and miserable. David had been giving me another pain medicine that Dr. Amy had given him for emergencies, but it wasn't helping much either.

As he looked into my eyes, he said, "If you can just make it to the hostel, Copper, I'm going to take you to see a veterinarian. We'll find out what's wrong. Can you do that? Can you walk that far?"

I didn't know how far it was, but I took a few steps toward the trail. David took my cue and followed.

"We'll go as slow as you need to, buddy. Just take your time."

I was glad to hear that and glad that it wasn't too long before we reached the hostel. As soon as we got there, David made a soft bed for me and called the veterinarian in Sharon, Connecticut. He got an appointment for the next day and the owner of the hostel agreed to drive us there. I was really looking forward to finding out what was wrong with me.

After another miserable night of sleep and breakfast the next morning, we drove off to see the new veterinarian. David was happy that they were able to squeeze me in for an examination, and it didn't take long for the veterinarian to share her suspicions.

"He is showing typical symptoms of Lyme disease, but we'll have to do a blood test to be sure," announced the veterinarian. "I'll give him a penicillin shot and some antibiotics to start treatment until I can get the lab results back".

David thanked the veterinarian and we headed back to the hostel where we waited for the results.

The next day when we entered the veterinarian's office, David could tell it was bad news. I knew by the look on his face. The test came back positive for Lyme disease.

"I've got a small supply of medicine that I can give you to get him started," said the veterinarian. "Then you'll have to get the rest at the pharmacy in town. He'll have to take the pills for a month with breakfast and dinner every day."

"How did he get this?" asked David.

"Let me guess," she answered. "I'd say he's been walking in lots of tall grasses along the trail, and I'd say you started removing lots of ticks when the heat of the summer began. Am I right?"

"Yes, sometimes, I would remove twenty or thirty at night and then have to remove about the same amount the next night. We first noticed them in Virginia, and then they got worse as we hiked through Maryland and Pennsylvania and on into New Jersey and New York. Once the weather warmed up, they appeared in every state that we passed through."

"That's how he got Lyme disease. Ticks are known carriers of the disease and it can make you feel terrible for quite a while. He's probably not going to bounce back from this very quickly."

Finally, we knew what was wrong.

I was in no shape to get back on the trail and the veterinarian said it would be best if I could take at least a week off from hiking and give the medicine time to do its job.

David had to come up with a plan pretty fast, so he decided to call a friend in Boston, Massachusetts and ask if we could visit for a few days. Vicki was an old friend and buddy who was happy to get to see David and see me. She agreed to let me rest in her home for a week while I got better.

NORTHBOUNDERS
Notes from the Appalachian Trail in Connecticut

- Ticks spread Lyme disease which makes you feel achy, especially in the joints of the body.
- David protected himself from ticks by wearing pants and gaiters. Gaiters are pieces of cloth put tightly around the legs and boots to keep ticks from getting to the skin. I wish they made them for dogs!
- People in Connecticut are very friendly.
- I am thankful for good veterinarians.
- The Appalachian Trail through Connecticut is about 148 miles.
- We have walked 1,330 miles and completed 61% of the Appalachian Trail.

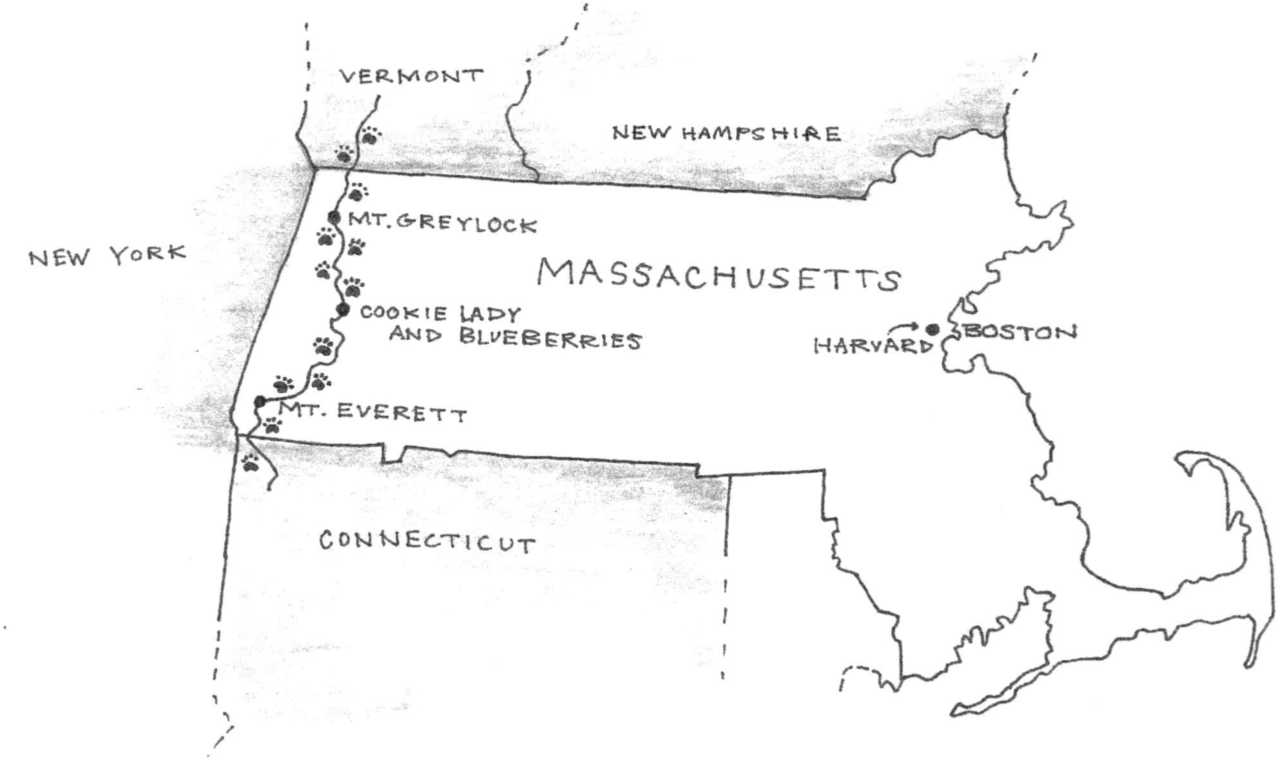
VERMONT
NEW HAMPSHIRE
NEW YORK
MT. GREYLOCK
MASSACHUSETTS
COOKIE LADY
AND BLUEBERRIES
HARVARD
BOSTON
MT. EVERETT
CONNECTICUT

CHAPTER 14
Massachusetts Mayhem

While I got better in Boston, David had fun adventures with Vicki. David told everybody that I was *recuperating*. I found out that it just means that I was trying to get better from my Lyme disease.

I lay around Vicki's house and slept for seven days as I waited for the medicine to make me well again. It began to help almost immediately. I was able to stand and walk on my own even though I still felt tired and weak.

David sat by my side, stroking my fur while he and Vicki talked. Vicki had to work during the week so that left David to get some rest and explore Boston on his own. When Vicki returned home at night, she would ask what sights he had seen during the day, and he enjoyed sharing his adventures with her. And of course, everything always comes back to food with hungry hikers, so he shared the news of his excellent meals and tasty treats that he found as he explored the city.

As our week came to an end and I was finally strong enough to leave, once again we had to determine how we could get back to the trail. David doesn't like to inconvenience people, so he always tries to figure things out on his own. This time, we had a problem which would require a bit of outside help. Or, as David said, "We have a conundrum." Sometimes I think he loves using those big words just to confuse me.

We had left the trail back in Connecticut and made our way to Boston in Massachusetts by getting rides from David's friends. Now we needed to get back to Connecticut. He came up with a plan to make a one-way car rental reservation and get us from Boston back to Connecticut. Unfortunately, when he tried to reserve one, there were no rental cars available. He thought and thought and then he remembered something. Moving trucks also can be rented one way. He called the moving truck company. Yes! They had a truck. Problem solved.

David was feeling very happy about getting back on the trail and decided to celebrate by taking a nice long shower before we left Vicki's house. Showers are a treasure when hiking the trail and he didn't know when he would have the opportunity for another one.

David knew that his backpack and smelly clothes had given Vicki's apartment a new smell and it wasn't the most pleasant odor. To remove the odor, he cracked the back door to let some fresh air in and headed for the shower. Before he entered the bathroom, he said, "You stay, Copper. I won't be long."

As I sat in the apartment waiting for him to finish showering, I noticed that the air was fairly cool and lots of new smells were coming into the apartment. David said to stay, but what could it hurt to go outside for a little bit, walk around, and check out what was nearby? I wouldn't be gone long and I'd be back before David got out of the shower.

I nudged the door open with my nose and then hooked a paw around the edge of the door to make an opening large enough to exit. Voila! I was on the street. The smells were so different here. They weren't at all like smells on the trail. And, goodness, there were so many cars! They zoomed by so fast that I couldn't cross the street. I decided it was best just to stay on the same side of the street as the apartment.

Just as I was beginning to enjoy myself, Vicki's landlord came walking by and yelled at me. "What are you doing on the street without a leash? Where is your owner?"

He knew that I was staying in Vicki's apartment, so he put his hands on my collar and pulled out his phone to make a call.

"Vicki, your friend's dog is out on the street without a leash, do you know why?"

"No," answered Vicki, "but I'll call David."

After that phone call, let's just say that things weren't good. The landlord was mad, Vicki was unhappy, and David was upset that I left the apartment and disobeyed him.

David had that look on his face that let me know that I was in trouble. Who knew that a little walk on the streets of Boston could make people so unhappy? I didn't know that all dogs had to be on a leash in the city!

I felt really bad that I had made Vicki, David, and the landlord so unhappy. Lately, it seems that I'm more trouble for David than I am pleasure. I tucked my tail between my legs and tried to be invisible.

David put the leash on my collar, and said thank you and goodbye to Vicki. We only had to walk a few miles before we had located the truck that would take us back to the trail. David signed a contract and off we went.

I had no idea what riding in this big moving rental truck would be like. Unfortunately, what it meant for me was a very narrow space between two front seats where I had to fit my long body. It was quite cramped, but I made it work. Every time David turned a corner, I wanted to yell *"Hey Buddy, I'm down here getting' squished into the sharpest parts of this truck!"* I was very thankful for our rest stops along the way to get out and stretch my legs.

David was having to navigate this big truck in an unfamiliar city where cars and trucks were everywhere. That was certainly a big change from hiking on the trail. Everything is slow out there. People take their time to enjoy each other's company, enjoy the views, and enjoy exploring whatever is just around the corner.

After a long and harrowing drive, we finally made it to Torrington, Connecticut where David dropped off the moving truck. The owner of Bearded Woods Hostel graciously agreed to pick us up in Torrington and take us back to the trail in Salisbury where David had to get off the trail because of my Lyme disease.

The man at the truck rental company didn't understand our trip at all.

"So you're hiking the Appalachian Trail, huh?" inquired the truck rental man.

"My dog and I are. This is Copper."

The truck rental man leaned down and I raised my paw to shake his hand.

"Well would you look at that? He's got some good manners."

He stood again without taking my paw, raised an eyebrow and said, "I don't understand why you drove from Boston to way out here. The trail isn't exactly nearby."

David explained about my sickness, needing to get off the trail, staying at a friend's house in Boston, and having to come back to Connecticut.

"But, why would you come south when you are trying to get to Maine which is north?" asked the man.

"Because I am a thru-hiker," replied David.

"What does that mean?" he asked sincerely.

"Well," began David. "I've always dreamed of being a true thru-hiker who hikes the entire length of the Appalachian Trail without missing any sections of the trail. If I skip the section between Connecticut and Massachusetts, I can't consider myself a thru-hiker."

"You still would have walked from Georgia to Maine, so what does it matter if you miss a 50 mile section? Who's going to know?"

"I'll know," said David. "I have to preserve the integrity of the thru-hiker. I could tell people that I hiked the Appalachian Trail from Georgia to Maine, but I couldn't honestly say that I was a thru-hiker. I have to be true to myself."

I laid down on the floor and tucked my head under my paws. That is something I will never be able to say. I can never be known as a thru-hiker. Even if I make it all the way to Maine, they won't let dogs hike the trail in the Smoky Mountains. That's a section that I will never get to see.

Still, I was proud of David's commitment, and I felt bad that I had made him miss a week of hiking. I was determined to stay healthy and be the best hiking buddy on the trail until we got to Maine.

The next day, we got a ride back to the trail and soon started hiking back towards the Massachusetts border. Since David wasn't quite sure how strong I was, he said that we would stop at Brassie Brook Shelter for the night. It was only a short distance away. But, when we stopped for a snack at the shelter, he could see that I was still energetic and ready to move on. So, we headed for Bear Mountain, the highest point in Connecticut. The views were beautiful, and the air was so fresh. It was good to be on the trail again.

We walked for days and met lots of new friends on the way: Dangerpants, Damselfly, Zeke, and Peaches just to name a few. All of our old friends were far ahead of us on the trail now, and moving too fast for us to catch up.

As the days wore on, we had a few things go wrong, but somehow people on the trail always made it better.

The first accident happened when David's head net fell out of his pocket on the trail somewhere and he was sorely missing it. The bugs were just as bad as ever.

Zeke, one of the new friends we met, was one of the friendliest hikers yet. He enjoyed a good story and loved to tell a good tale as well. He insisted on sharing his snacks and even volunteered to create a makeshift fan to keep the bugs off of everybody. The bugs were swarming in droves.

As David was talking to Zeke around the campfire and trying to keep away the bugs, Zeke said, "You should get a head net next time you are in town to help keep the bugs off of your face."

"I had one," replied David. "I got hot while climbing Mt. Everett, so I took it off and put it in my pocket. Somehow it fell out. I sure do miss it though."

"Did it look like this?" asked Zeke as he held the head net up.

"Exactly like that."

"Then it's yours," said Zeke, as he passed it to him.

"No, I can't take that. You'll need it."

"It's not mine," replied Zeke. "I found it on top of Mt. Everett. I've been keeping it in my pocket just waiting to return it to its owner. I must confess that I did wear it a few times when the bugs got really bad."

David immediately declared Zeke to be the nicest person on the trail for he had been missing that head net terribly.

The second accident happened almost immediately after we got back on the trail. The pad that protected the straps on my backpack somehow fell off and neither of us noticed. David thinks that it must have fallen off as he was removing it from my back and we just didn't see it happen. The next morning when David started to put my pack on he said, "Oh no, Copper! Your padding is missing on your straps. You stay here and let me look around the shelter."

He looked and looked but couldn't find it. I sniffed around the area trying to find something that had my scent on it. But *everything* smelled like me, so my superior nose couldn't help us find it either.

David gave up and made a makeshift pad out of a small towel he had, and we headed off down the trail. It worked, but it wasn't nearly as comfortable as the pad.

Once again, a trail friend came through. Another hiker had found it and carried it to the next shelter to the north and put it under the table. When we arrived at the shelter, there it was. To top off the night, some hikers had left self-heating meals in a bear box for any hikers who wished to have them for dinner. What a find!

All in all, it had been a great few days of hiking even with the things that had gotten lost and found along the way.

The most exciting thing for David on our hike this week was the U-Pick Blueberry Farm that we visited. He got so excited picking berries that I had a tough time keeping up with him just to get there. That boy does love berries! He was just as enthusiastic about the blueberries as he was the blackberries in Pennsylvania.

To top it all off, there was the famous Cookie Lady right there at the farm. She baked cookies for all the hikers and set them on the porch where hikers were welcome to take one. What a nice idea and a nice lady. When we finally left, he was walking very quickly, whistling a tune, and stopping every few feet to give me some ear scratches. I think he was pleased, and so was I, because every time David gets a snack, he gives me one too. It's different from his, but I'll take a meaty biscuit over a blueberry any day of the week.

"You know what I'm going to have for dinner, Copper?" David asked, practically bounding down the trail.

I was pretty sure I knew what he would say next.

"Blueberries!" he continued. "And guess what I'm going to have for dessert?"

Blueberries?

"Blueberries! I might even have blueberries for breakfast."

And he did! His entire dinner consisted of blueberries. He's weird! I'll stick with my kibble, I think.

We spent the next few days following the trail through Massachusetts, climbing Mt. Greylock (a tough climb), and enjoying new trail friends. I was healthy now and keeping up with David, but I was still exhausted at night. We needed to make up for lost time and move on into the next state of Vermont. I was doing my best to keep up, but I was still having doubts about finishing the trail. If Zeke's tales were true, we had a hard road ahead of us.

Notes from the Appalachian Trail in Massachusetts

- Vicki is a good friend to let me stay and get better from Lyme disease.
- Lyme disease can make you very weak. Or as David says with his big words, "It's debilitating."
- Trail friends are the best. They leave nothing on the trail and carry lost and found items forward hoping to find the owner.
- Riding in a moving truck can be an inexpensive way to travel in rural areas, but it is cramped and NOT FUN for a dog!
- The Appalachian Trail through Massachusetts is about 91 miles.
- We have walked 1,427 miles and completed 65% of the Appalachian Trail.

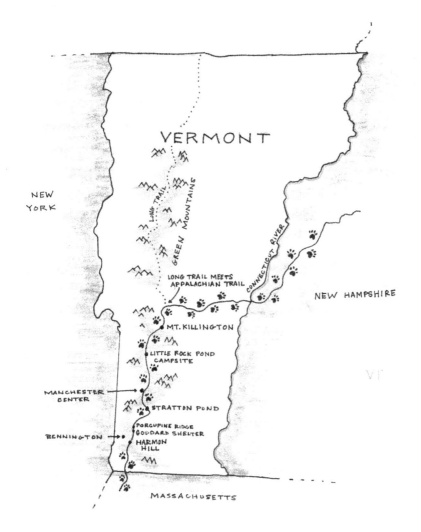

VERMONT

NEW
YORK

LONG TRAIL

GREEN MOUNTAINS

CONNECTICUT RIVER

LONG TRAIL MEETS
APPALACHIAN TRAIL

NEW HAMPSHIRE

MT. KILLINGTON

LITTLE ROCK POND
CAMPSITE

MANCHESTER
CENTER

STRATTON POND

PORCUPINE RIDGE
GODDARD SHELTER

BENNINGTON

HARMON
HILL

MASSACHUSETTS

CHAPTER 15
Vermont Vistas

As soon as we crossed into Vermont we immediately started climbing. It was only a short hike from where we spent the night before I heard David say, "We're in Vermont and will soon be hiking through the Green Mountains." He was very excited to cross the border and see a new state.

He was walking and talking to Cody Coyote, whom he'd met a few days before on the trail. As we climbed the hill and I listened to them talk, I reflected on how fun it is to meet back up with friends that you make on the trail. That's a big part of trail life.

"I'm glad to see some more 4,000 foot mountains," said Cody Coyote as he pulled his long legs up the mountain.

"Me too," said David. "We haven't seen hills this high since Virginia. They should be a breeze since our legs are so much stronger now."

"I know mine are," answered Cody Coyote. "And yours look like tree trunks! They should be *really* strong!"

David laughed and said, "Copper's upper legs are like rocks. He's gotten lean and become a muscle machine. Right, Copper?"

I ran ahead of David and Cody Coyote to show off my new physique. I had become very muscular and my strong muscles made climbing up those 4,000 footers a lot easier than when we first started out.

"He sure looks strong," said Cody Coyote. "I wonder if Vermont is going to be much longer and harder for us than Massachusetts."

"I think so. In fact, it's almost twice as long. I was looking at the map last night and discovered that the Appalachian Trail and the Long Trail come together as one for about 100 miles. Then there will be a fork in the road. If we go straight, the Long Trail will take us into Canada. If we take the fork, we will continue on the A.T. to Maine."

"Well, this hiker is taking the fork and heading straight for Maine," proclaimed Cody Coyote. "I've been out here walking for five months with a goal of climbing Mt. Katahdin in Maine. I'm not about to change that goal now."

"I agree," said David as he knelt to give me a warm hug and ear scratches. "Copper and I feel the same way. We need to keep our eyes on the prize."

"In fact, I'm so excited about moving on towards Maine that I think I'm going to jog for a little bit. I'll see you two on down the trail."

He bent down to give me a hug and then he took off running.

At first, the terrain looked the same. Everything looked like Massachusetts except the hills were higher. Slowly, the scenery began to change into something spectacular. Vermont was truly one of the most beautiful states we had been through. It was green with wildflowers everywhere.

David had talked quite a bit about having to hike through mud in Vermont but we hadn't seen any yet, and we were happy about that. My short legs and deep mud do not go together very well. It would be just as bad as trying to slush through the snow like I had to do back in North Carolina. That is *not* a pleasant memory. I was trying to get that horrible image out of my mind when I heard David talking to somebody.

"Hi," said David, to a female hiker as she bounded down the hill. "How goes the Southbounding life?"

"Great!" answered the hiker. "I've made it through Maine and New Hampshire and now I'm almost through Vermont and headed to Georgia. By the way, I'm Dimples. Who is that beautiful dog?"

"His name is Copper, and he's hiking the trail with me. My name is Blast. It's easy to see how you got your trail name."

She laughed, extended her hand to David, and then turned to gaze at me, asking, "Is it okay if I pet Copper?"

"Sure," answered David. "He loves the attention and especially likes scratches behind the ears and belly rubs."

Dimples laughed. "My dog does too. I said goodbye to my dog when I left home in Maine, and I've missed him every day that I've been out here. I wish I had made the choice to bring him along, but I just wasn't sure he could make it. Jackson and Copper would have liked each other."

"I felt the same way because of Copper's age. He's ten years old."

"No way! He seems so agile and he walks like a young dog. He looks great!"

I stood at attention with my head held high and offered my paw for her to shake.

"Awwww," said Dimples as she reached down to shake my paw. "Jackson does the same thing. Now, I *really* miss him."

"Well," said David. "He's had his share of troubles on the trail, but he just keeps on going. He amazes me. He's got the hiker spirit, I guess."

"By the way, since you've already hiked through most of Vermont, did you have to hike a good bit in the mud? The hikers say that Vermont only has two seasons: winter and mud season. I've even read tales of hikers losing their boots in the mud because it actually sucked their boots off their feet."

I didn't like the sound of that! I remember my boots getting sucked off by the snow. It sounded even worse having them sucked off by the mud.

"Yeah, I actually know some hikers who hiked last year and had that happen. But it seems that the heat wave caused the water to dry up almost as fast as the snow melted this year. They had some mud earlier, but it seems to be gone now. Everything I've hiked through has been beautiful and green. It looks like Vermont will have three seasons this year: winter, mud, and summer," said Dimples.

"Great," replied David. "Thanks for the info! It was nice to meet you, Dimples. Hope you make it all the way to Georgia."

Throughout the southern half of Vermont, the mud stayed away, the views were beautiful, and the climbs were fairly easy. When we climbed to the top of Harmon Hill, the last hill before the town of Bennington, David stopped and began picking something from a tree and popping it into his mouth. I couldn't tell what it was, but it was red. He was moaning and saying, "Mmmmm, these are so good!" I had heard those words many times on this hike. I don't think there is a single food that boy doesn't like.

As he swallowed, he turned to me and said, "Look, Copper, a wild cherry tree. I need one of these in our yard back home. I love cherries."

While David continued to sample the cherries, I checked out the rest of the area. David kept popping cherries and then moaning because they tasted so good, so it wasn't hard to explore and still know that he was in the area. When he had finally had his fill, he stated how nice it was that free food was growing wild right beside the trail. He sure does love his snacks. First, it was blackberries, then it was blueberries, and now cherries.

I couldn't get too excited about berries, but if steak grew on the side of the trail, I would be ecstatic!

We took it easy crossing Porcupine Ridge on our way to Goddard Shelter where we had planned to spend the night. David was checking all the vegetation on the trail and looking for more berries to pick for breakfast. As we rounded the corner, I caught the scent of some hikers and heard two new voices chatting happily and laughing.

As we passed by, one of the new voices yelled, "Hey, come over here! Look, what we found."

"What is it?" asked David

"We're not going to tell you, you have to see this for yourself," answered the other voice.

As we walked toward the voices, we immediately saw the objects of their happiness.

"Whoa." said David. "So. Many. Apples. How did you two see these from the trail? They are a little hard to spot from back there."

"Speck has eagle eyes when it comes to finding food on the trail. By the way, I'm Dangerpants"

"I'm Blast," said David, "and this is Copper." He pulled an apple from a low-hanging limb, took a bite, and said, "I'm glad you stopped us. These are some crispy apples--and just a little bit sour, just like I like them. By the way, how did you get such interesting trail names?"

Dangerpants responded first, "Well, it's sort of embarrassing, but I'll tell you. I got mine early in my hike when I was sitting around a fire one night and a big spark from the fire landed on my pants. It startled me, so I jumped up, started dancing around, and slapping at my pants to put out the fire." She started pantomiming the dancing and slapping as she spoke. "Everybody started laughing at how funny I looked and somebody yelled, 'Danger! Pants on fire!' Then someone else yelled, 'That's it. That's your trail name. Dangerpants!' So that's who I am now."

When David finally stopped laughing at the show, he said "That's a story for the ages! How about you, Speck? How did you get your trail name?"

She quietly responded, "I've been section hiking the A.T. for several years and every time I get back on the trail, I always feel that

I'm just a little speck on the earth. The world seems so big and amazing out here on the trail."

"I agree with that," said David.

I did too. I related to Speck. That's how I feel on the trail. I seem so small and the world around me seems really big. There's so much exploring to do.

David continued to munch on his apple and then decided to pull a piece of Vermont cheese from his pack to eat on top of the apple. It was his new favorite snack.

Speck noticed his snack and said, " I see you like apples and cheese together. Have you ever had a Vermonster?"

"No," answered David. "What's that?"

"It's a divine sandwich made with Vermont cheddar cheese, Vermont apples and Vermont ham, with mustard on a hoagie roll." answered Speck. "You want to try one? I bought three of them and had them cut into pieces just so I could share them. Here, take a piece."

"Mmmmmm," moaned David as he took his first bite. "This is my new favorite sandwich. My mouth is crying 'more, more, more!'"

"I told you," said Speck. "They're addictive! Here, have another piece."

David took the second piece, ate most of it and then leaned down to give me a small bite. Speck was right. It was good stuff!

While Speck and Dangerpants picked a few apples to take with them, I lazed under the shade of the apple tree. When they decided it was time to move on down the trail, they said, "Bye David. Bye Copper, we'll see you later." They leaned over and gave me a few rubs on the head and then they were gone.

"Copper, come over here," said David. "We need to take some of these with us, too."

He started picking apples and putting them in *my* backpack. He even counted them as he dropped them in.

"...17, 18, 19, 20. Perfect," he declared. "That should last me awhile and give us some to share. Thanks for taking them for me, little buddy!"

I rolled my eyes and thought, *No problem, David. Happy to be of service. I'd love to carry 1/10th of my body weight in apples which aren't even for me!*

Just for the record, Vermont was full of apple trees and yes, I was *always* the carrier of the apples.

Vermont proved to have perfect hiking weather, and one of my favorite climbs (even with a pack full of apples) was the climb up Mt. Killington. I like climbing *up* because I am low to the ground and can climb faster than David. He's faster going *down* because I am more cautious. When we are going up, I usually get to lead. Mt. Killington was a little different. Because the mountain had sheer vertical sections and there were so many paths to choose from, David had to help me choose. It sounds easy, but picking the easiest path to get up the mountain can be tricky. I'm pretty good at it, but sometimes it takes me a while to figure it out. This was one of those times. Some paths came to a dead end. Others led to overgrown brush and briars. Others were very rocky with sharp stones. The path I chose this time would have led me off the side of a mountain if David hadn't been paying attention. He called me back to the path he had chosen and led me straight up.

Once we were over the mountain, we quickly came to a road crossing followed by a slow easy climb up to the Little Rock Pond Campsite. David had decided that we would stop here for the night and went to talk to the caretaker. He chose a camping spot and then noticed that there was a canoe on the property.

"Excuse me, sir." said David. "I noticed that there is a canoe down by the water. May I rent it?"

"It's there for anyone to use," replied the caretaker. "Take a ride and explore a little bit if you want to."

David winked at me, smiled, and said, "How would you like to take your very first canoe ride, Copper?"

He knows that I'm always up for an adventure, so I quickly ran to the canoe and put my paw on the paddle.

"Hop in," he said. "Let's see how you like canoeing."

I leapt into the canoe, and the boat rocked violently from side to side with water gushing in over the front, the back, and both sides. It was a little scary and it was difficult to keep my balance. I jumped back onto the shore before I could fall in the water.

"I didn't mean to *literally* hop in, Copper. I just meant to get in the canoe."

David scooped the water out of the canoe with a plastic scoop left in the bottom for just that purpose, then grabbed the sides to keep it from rocking. "Alright, boy, go on up to the front and lie down. You can be our boat captain, but you've got to keep very still, or the boat will tip over, and we'll both be in the water."

I did as he said, and David climbed in and rowed us all the way across the pond. I was just as still as I could be. It felt a little funny at first, like maybe the canoe *was* going to turn over, but then I got used to the feeling and I liked it.

Floating along in the canoe, I could see fish jumping, ducks swimming and flying overhead, and steep rocks looming all around the edges of the pond. Suddenly, a huge fish jumped out of the water and high into the air and landed back in the water with a big splash. *What kind of fish is that?* I thought *And where is it going?* Curious, I bounded over the canoe seat towards the back to take a closer look at the fish. Just as I landed, I lost my balance and fell hard on top of David forcing him over the side edge of the canoe. As he tried to sit back up, I lost my balance again and ended up shoving us both back to the side with a bug thud. The sudden tilt of the boat under our weight was too much. In the blink of an eye, the canoe flipped and we were under water.

I struggled to get out from under the canoe and came up sputtering. When I realized I was okay, I started looking for David to be sure he was okay. I swam around the canoe two or three times looking for him. Where was he? Why wasn't he coming up out of the water?

With David out of sight and my own legs tiring, I decided to swim to shore. Maybe I could see him from there. As I got to shore, I ran up and down the edge of the pond trying to catch a glimpse of his head, his shirt, anything to show me where he was. He was nowhere in sight, but the canoe was moving slowly toward me. I continued to run back and forth, barking, and trying to get David to answer me or tell me to be quiet or something. I heard nothing. Not a sound.

As the canoe continued floating slowly toward me, again I searched each side of it looking for David. I watched as the nose of the canoe touched land and stayed there. I ran to the left to look one more time and ran right into some legs…David's legs. How did he do that? How did he appear out of nowhere? I was watching the boat the whole time.

David came out of the water laughing. He reached down, patted my wet head and said, "You took the long way buddy."

He squatted beside me, turned my head to the right and said, "See that rock over there. When the canoe flipped, I just popped up out of the water, swam a few feet, climbed on that rock and was back on dry land. All I had to do was walk over here to get you and the canoe". He let out another hearty laugh, gave me a little ear tug and went to scoop the water out and turn the canoe right side up.

That wasn't nice of him. He scared me!

We sat on the sand at the edge of the pond enjoying the rest of the afternoon. Just as the sun slipped behind the mountain, David said, "I guess we better get back to camp, cook some dinner, and go to sleep. We have a big week ahead of us. The rest of Vermont won't be that hard, but I hear it's going to rain a lot. If we can stay warm and make it through all that wetness, we can rest and refresh in Hanover. Before we can do that, though, we have to get out of the Green Mountains, get to the Connecticut River, and cross it, leaving Vermont behind us. Waiting for us in New Hampshire will be the White Mountains, some of the highest and most deadly mountains of our trip."

Notes from the Appalachian Trail in Vermont

- Apples and cherries grow wild in Vermont.
- Canoes are fun to ride in as long as I am very still. Otherwise, we land in the water.
- David has a new favorite food: Vermont Cheddar cheese. He loves to eat it with apples he finds on the trail. I like it too, but he never wants to share!
- The Vermonster is an awesome sandwich!
- The Appalachian Trail through Vermont is about 150 miles.
- We have walked 1577 miles and completed 72% of the Appalachian Trail.

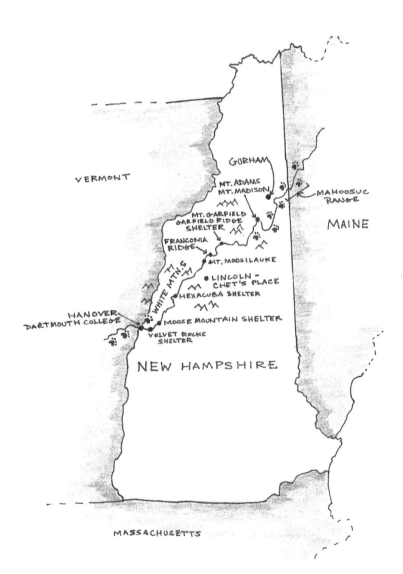

VERMONT

GORHAM

MT. ADAMS
MT. MADISON

MAHOOSUC
RANGE

MT. GARFIELD
GARFIELD RIDGE
SHELTER

MAINE

FRANCONIA
RIDGE

MT. MOOSILAUKE

WHITE MTN.S

LINCOLN ~
CHET'S PLACE

HEXACUBA SHELTER

HANOVER
DARTMOUTH COLLEGE

MOOSE MOUNTAIN SHELTER

VELVET ROCKS
SHELTER

NEW HAMPSHIRE

MASSACHUSETTS

CHAPTER 16
Novelty in New Hampshire

"This sign says we are 431 miles from the end of the trail," announced David as he rubbed my head. "We've come a long way together, my friend."

As quickly as we entered New Hampshire, we found ourselves in the town of Hanover. The A.T. goes straight through downtown Hanover to Dartmouth College, whose most famous graduate is Dr. Seuss. David's little sister, Mikella, used to lay on her bedroom floor beside me and read the Dr. Seuss stories aloud. I can still hear her reading about green eggs and ham, the cat in the hat, and Mr. Brown who moos. Mikella would say, "Mr. Brown can moo, can you?" I never did learn how to do that.

As we left Hanover and continued on our way towards Moose Mountain, the trail became level. We went around wetlands, across roads, and sometimes past houses. The weather was perfect for hiking and we were enjoying our stroll. When we reentered the woods and started our slow climb up to Velvet Rocks through a field of tall grass, David yelled, "Ouch!" and began shaking his hand violently.

He held it tightly to his chest and as I came up to make sure he was okay, he said, "It's okay, boy. I just got stung by a wasp. It hurts, but I'll be fine."

He showed me the red sting and I licked his wound to make it better. Wasps don't seem to bother me. If they do, I snap them between my jaws and eat them!

We enjoyed the relatively easy start to New Hampshire and spent our first days there walking and talking with Speck and Dangerpants who had rejoined us on the trail. We ended our night taking sunset pictures atop Mt. Smarts and walking together to Moose Mountain Shelter where we spent our first night in New Hampshire.

While eating dinner, David planned the next few days of hiking and questioned Dangerpants about the next shelter.

"Why do they call the next shelter Hexacuba?"

"Because it has six sides. You know, like a hexagon. And since we are climbing toward Mt. Cube, they named it Hexacuba."

"Makes total sense," said David. "I knew it had something to do with six, but I haven't seen a six-sided shelter yet. This one should be totally different."

When we got to the shelter, he said, "Wow! This could probably sleep 20 people! What a cool shelter."

David found a place for his sleeping pad and sleeping bag inside and unrolled it to make his bed for the night. He found a place for me to sleep outside and then made our dinner. He always fed me first since his dinner takes longer to get ready. I fell asleep in a matter of minutes listening to the hikers as they ate and reminisced about their day.

After a sunrise breakfast the next morning, we continued our hike into what we were told by fellow hikers would be a challenging part of the trail. It wasn't long before we reached Mt. Moosilauke, the first mountain in the White Mountains section of the trail to reach over 4,000 feet.

"Copper, this section is going to be tough," David told me. "We've got to go straight up the side of this slippery cascade, and the only way up for both of us is using these wooden blocks bolted into these rocks. We are going to have to use them for traction. Otherwise, we are going to slip and go tumbling down the mountain. It's going to take teamwork to get up and over this mountain, buddy."

I was very thankful for those blocks of wood to give me traction on the inclines and very thankful for David's help. Eventually, the trail leveled out and became a path of tiny rocks which cut into the pads of my paws incessantly. This was a tough day of hiking. It took us from dawn to dusk to climb and descend that mountain, and we worked for every inch of its 4,803 feet.

After our climb over Mt. Moosilauke, we got a ride from a trail angel into the town of Lincoln. David knew that he had to acquire some different gear. We were warned that we might encounter some of the coldest and worst weather of our trip through the White Mountains, so David had arranged for his mom to send his winter gear to the Lincoln, New Hampshire post office. He also had to buy a new pair of boots. His were falling apart; he had actually taped them back together with duct tape. If he'd just hike barefoot like me, he'd save a lot of money!

We never knew exactly what day we would arrive in a city so the post office would hold the package for us as long as his mom addressed it to David and wrote, *Please HOLD for Thru-Hiker.* This time she had sent his tent, his zero-degree sleeping bag, his sleeping pad, and some winter clothing including his hat and gloves. This was the same trail-proven gear that we were using at the beginning of this hike, so we knew we'd be okay even if the temperature dropped below freezing.

David took the winter gear out of the box, along with some new treats for me, and then he packed the hammock and his warm weather gear inside the box and sent it back home. David said we were now ready for whatever weather would come our way. I was ready to taste those new snacks!

We set out walking with our winter gear safely packed away and found our way to a shelter for the evening. Upon waking the next morning, we heard the ping, ping, ping of the rain on the roof. It looked as though the unpredictable weather of New Hampshire had begun. David was undeterred. He crawled out of his sleeping bag, put on his rain clothes, and we headed for the trail. It was a long day's hike from Kinsman Notch to Eliza Brook shelter. It was uphill the whole way out of the notch (a passage between two mountains) except for a very brief downhill before we started climbing Mt. Wolf.

Along the ridge of Mt. Wolf, there was nothing but tall fir trees and piles of deep fluffy moss padding the ground. It felt like soft fluffy cotton with cool threads of grass woven among the fibers. It was a welcome relief from the ever-present rocks on the trail. I took a little time to prance around and roll in it to revel in this new find on the trail. I sure wish the *whole* trail was made of this stuff!

David laughed as he watched me enjoy the fluffy new turf. After a few minutes of fun, David said, "Come on Copper. We've got to get to the shelter. I've got a treat for you."

When we arrived at Eliza Brook shelter, David sat down out of the rain, pulled me into the empty shelter, hugged me close and said, "You know what today is, right Copper? We are 75% done with our hike." I watched as he reached into his pack and pulled out a slightly smashed cake that he had bought back in Lincoln for this very celebration. I laid my paw on his leg, looked up expectantly, and watched patiently as he ate ¾ of a cake.

"It had to be done, Copper. It's a tradition now!" said David as he licked his fingers. "The next time you see me eat cake, we will be finished hiking the trail and that means I'll have to eat the whole thing."

He gave me a treat to celebrate with him and then he leaned back, patted his belly, and took a nap. These hiker traditions are quite funny to watch. David would never consider eating more than one piece of cake at home. But, knowing how many calories it takes to climb these mountains, he had no second thoughts about devouring so much cake. He was stuffed and not moving, so we enjoyed a quiet and uneventful, if rainy, night at the shelter.

We were thankful for a good night's rest because the next section of trail was tough. We were climbing Mt. Kinsman straight up bare rock faces and over ledges. There was no way that I could leap onto them or even begin to find a way to climb up on them. David found himself having to climb halfway up a crack in the rock, plant his feet on either side of the crack, place one hand in the crack, squat and grab the handle on my pack and lift me up and over onto the ledge all while wearing a 20lb. pack. He had to do this over and over again. I don't know how he did it. It must be thanks to those legs that Cody Coyote called "tree trunks". David was concerned about hurting me and kept checking to make sure I was okay. It didn't hurt at all. I was just worried about how much trouble I was causing David trying to get me over each big rock. I was upset with myself that I didn't have the physical strength or athleticism to complete this hike on my own. Time after time, David had to stop and haul me over another ledge.

When there was a possibility for a choice, David always gave me an opportunity to try to find a path that was best for me. Most of the time I found a good path, but because of my short legs, there are just some things I can't do. This mountain was challenging. Finally, we made it over Mt. Kinsman and down to Kinsman Pond Shelter.

"Copper, you were quite a trooper back there," said David. "That was some tough terrain. The sad news is that after five hours and all that work, we've only gone two and a half miles. Look at us, we're both exhausted!"

I knew that he could have gone so much further if it hadn't been for me. I could tell that he was tired and frustrated. I'm just hoping that he doesn't make me get off the trail and send me back home. I know I'm slowing him down but I *really* want to finish this hike with him. I also know that he can't keep spending half a day only going 2.5 miles either. We usually average 12-15 miles a day.

Kinsman Pond was beautiful, and even though it was cool, I wanted to take a dip in the water while David had a late lunch. David unbuckled my backpack, and I waded into the clear cool water. We stayed there and rested a bit and then gathered our things. David picked up a large branch that would make a good hiking stick to steady himself in preparation for our trek through the toughest terrain of New Hampshire. As the sun set, we walked in silence to Liberty Springs campground. We arrived sometime after dark, and rain had already started falling.

We found a site, and I bent over my dinner to try to keep the rain off it while I ate. David hurried to get his tent set up and us inside before it started really pouring. It turned out the tent had lost its waterproofing, and *everything* got wet. It rained all night and into the morning and showed no signs of letting up. That did not deter David. He was focused on a mission. He packed up our wet gear, put on our wet backpacks and headed towards the ridge.

The rain, which had let up somewhat, returned in full force as the ridge was encompassed by a cloud. The wind blew so forcefully that it was really hard to walk. I was having trouble just standing up. This was the infamous weather of the White Mountains! We were supposed to have awesome views from Franconia Ridge, but it was too foggy to see anything. The rain blinded us as we walked through it and the wind knocked us backwards. Combine the fog, the rain, the wind, and the difficulty of the climb, to get nothing short of misery. This was torture!

The rain in and on my pack had made it terribly heavy, and it rubbed against my skin with every step I took. It wasn't long before the chafing became painful. The only things in my pack were my food and my leash but the weight of the water made it heavier than it had been since David had finally stopped filling it with apples. It wouldn't move right and the tight, wet straps felt like sandpaper. I continued on as best I could, and then I just couldn't take it anymore. I sat down on the side of the trail and began chewing on the straps that were irritating me. I needed some relief! I would yank on the straps to try to ease the chafing, and then run for a bit to catch up before David got out of sight.

We finally summited Mt. Lafayette, the highest peak of the ridge, over 5,000 feet above sea level, where the weather continued to rage. Up there above the tree line, we were in the clouds--cold, soaking wet, and miserable.

Finally, as I climbed up along Franconia Ridge, I was able to rub against the rocks to move the pack enough to get some relief. But, as I began walking again, I realized that I had chewed the straps a little too much and the pack fell to the ground. David had no way of knowing that the pack had fallen on the trail and I had no way to alert him. He was the leader for the day, I was the follower, and we were walking in the fog. I caught up to him and nudged him. He didn't notice.

As the rain fell harder and the wind whipped around us, two hikers finally came up behind David and said, "Hey, is that your dog's pack back there?"

David looked down at me and concluded, "Yes, I guess it is. Thanks."

He turned around and started back along the ridge to retrieve it.

"Copper, how did you get that pack off?"

He was *not* happy with me. As we walked, he gave me the silent treatment and totally ignored me. I hated when he did that because that's how I knew he was really angry. It was hard enough to climb the mountain once without having to backtrack. He was not happy about having to do it twice in this terrible weather.

The pack was laying by the rocks where it had slid to the ground. Picking it up and shaking the water and dirt off, he tried to put it back on me. That's when he realized what I'd done.

"Copper, why did you chew through these straps? I can't put it on you until it gets fixed. I can't even hook it to my backpack. I guess I'll just carry it in my hand."

He gave me more of the silent treatment as we walked. He was *really* unhappy now.

As I watched David trying desperately to manage everything in this weather, I began to feel really guilty. Once again, I was causing extra work for him. He was now walking with *his* water-drenched pack, *my* water-drenched pack, and a hiking stick while lifting my considerable mass over ledges that were impossible for me to climb. I knew he was tired from climbing and carrying extra weight. Once again, I could only hope that he was not silently seething inside and plotting a plan to leave me with someone while he finished the hike without me.

As we summited Mt. Lafayette for the second time, our already rotten day got worse. The rain got heavier and the wind got stronger. It was beyond miserable. There was nowhere to get out of the driving rain. All along the side of Mt. Lafayette, the trail went around the edge of a sheer, steep rock slab with water rushing down in streams.

David had to work his way around the edge of it, gripping the corners of boulders with his one free hand, to keep from sliding down it. I had no idea what to do in this area. I stayed close to David and he led me down and out of danger.

For the first time on the trail, I had real doubts as to whether I could finish it. The trail just didn't make sense anymore. Hiking the trail was becoming impossible for me, and the weather was trying my patience and skills.

When we finally got back below the tree line and the weather calmed down, David sat down on a rock, took out his needle and thread and began stitching up the pack. He always carried a needle and thread to be prepared for any rips or tears in clothing or gear.

"So Copper, did the pack just get too heavy for you?" David asked as he stitched the strap back into place.

I looked up at him with pleading eyes, willing him to understand my plight and my fear.

He looked at me and said, "Next time, I'll take *my* pack off and let *you* carry it!"

I tucked my head under his legs. I felt terrible about making him carry my pack, and now he was having to spend time to fix what I'd torn up. It had been a tough day.

When the pack was sewn back together, David squeezed and emptied any leftover water and put it on my back. It felt fine now. It was wet but at least it wasn't full of water.

We trudged on down the trail, climbed over Mt. Garfield and down to Garfield Ridge shelter. This section was even more miserable than Franconia Ridge. We spent the rest of the day scaling rock cliffs, finding cracks in ledges for climbing, and trying desperately to summit the mountain.

When we finally summited, we headed for the shelter where David hung all of our stuff up to dry and hoped for clearer days and better hiking the next day, but it wasn't to be. The weather was getting worse and the White Mountains are not to be taken lightly. Many people have died in those mountains because they believed they could outlast the bad weather. David wasn't going to take any chances with himself or with me. We got out of there.

We took a side trail down the mountain to a public road and got a ride from a friend we had met earlier in Lincoln. He took us back to Chet's Place, a hostel that allowed dogs to stay inside. Chet was a hiker and his love for the trail is so strong that he turned part of his house into a hiker hostel where weary hikers could rest before or after hiking through the White Mountains.

When we arrived at Chet's Place, I managed to eat dinner and then just slept and slept and slept. I was really weary and had no interest in visiting with the other hikers. I was losing what David had called my hiker spirit. My joints were aching and I was just *tired*.

We ended up having to stay at Chet's Place for a few days because the weather in the White Mountains was terrible. It was only September—not yet winter—but the White Mountains are very unpredictable. It could be horrible weather one day and beautiful hiking weather the next. David checked the weather every day and finally it cleared up. The weather report said things were looking good for hiking.

As David prepared our packs to go, a hiker friend who was resting up at Chet's said, "Why don't you just leave Copper here with me and let him rest. He's an old man, you know. You can go ahead and hike for a few days, climb the highest peak, Mt. Washington, and then catch a ride back here and pick him up. I'd love to have him spend a few days with me and give him a chance to rest. We'll rest up together."

I pleaded with my eyes—*No, David, please don't go without me. If I can just rest for a few more days, I'll have my strength and energy back. Climbing those rugged mountains wore me out. I know you are tired too. Stay with me!*

"I think it is best to go on without him. After all, he is almost 11 years old. He's been on quite a hike for such an old dog, and he's been amazing. Maybe I do need to leave him here with you, but I hate to burden you."

"It would be my pleasure to have this fine dog stay with me and keep me company. I'm sure the other hikers will enjoy having a furry friend around too. You go on ahead and climb Mt. Washington."

So, it was set. David would leave me at Chet's Place and climb Mt. Washington. The plan was for him to come back for me before he climbed Mt. Adams and continued on into Maine, but I had my doubts. Why would he climb and hike some of the most treacherous terrain and then turn around and come back to get a dog who can't keep up, can't climb, keeps getting sick, destroys his pack, gets sprayed by skunks, and offers nothing of value in return. There is absolutely no joy in having me around anymore. I'm not a companion—I'm a burden.

I moped around for the next few days and was not at all my usual self. The ear scratches from the hikers, the offers to sleep curled up with me at night, and the endless offers of treats meant nothing to me. All I wanted was for David to come back to get me. I was using all of my energy to *will* him back to me.

Lying in the sun one afternoon after what seemed a very long time since David left, I caught a familiar scent. It was a scent I loved and had sorely missed. I looked up just in time to see David bounding up Chet's driveway, asking "Where's my buddy? Where's my Copper dog?"

He came back! I couldn't believe it. David came back! I leapt up off the floor, ran to his arms, stretched as far as I could, and placed my paws on his shoulders so I could be eye to eye with him. I needed him to see in my eyes how much I missed him and needed him. I couldn't get enough of his scent, his touch, and the very sight of him. He really came back. It had worked. I had willed him back to me.

"Do you think you're ready to go on, Copper?" he asked. "I saved something very special for you to see. You're going to be very impressed with the views from Mt. Adams."

I knew that he came back to give me one last chance to prove myself. I would *not* let him down. No more sickness, no more weakness, no trouble for David. This was it. We are finishing this together and I *will* be strong.

I was so glad to hear his voice and to see that he had made it through those mountains safely. He was going to spend the night, and we would start out together the next morning. I was ready to go, and I was feeling good. We would be a hiking team again!

When we woke up the next morning, the weather was warm and it was a sunny day. I was up early and ready to go. Before leaving Chet's Place, David took care to get both of our packs organized. Then, we headed out to climb Mt. Madison and Mt. Adams.

The trail started as a very wide road paved with dead leaves and scattered with small rocks. It was really easy walking and we met lots of hikers on the way. It was good to be back among them as they patted my head, asked David my name, and asked lots of questions about our trip together.

The trail got tougher the following morning. It was full of uneven rocks which really tore at the pads of my paws. From the rocky paths, we crossed swollen rivers and streams, which I had to pick my way through carefully to make it to the other side. As we found the trail again, it ran into more ledges where I was forced to find a path. Then, we were back to the rocky uneven terrain.

Picking my path to the top of Mt. Adams became tougher and tougher. Every path that I tried either ended in a ledge too high to climb or ended in a dead end rock wall. It seemed that I was walking miles and getting nowhere. David was able to go straight up because he could pull himself up and over ledges. That wasn't an option for me, so David sometimes had to bodily lift me onto the next ledge.

Finally, with David's help, I made it to the highest point of Mt. Adams.

The view was incredible, but I was worn out from my exhausting climb. Thankfully, as we headed down the mountain, it looked as though it would be an easy walk to the shelter.

Wrong. A few minutes later we were looking at another sheer rock wall which again was impossible for me to climb. The hand-over-hand method was the official way to climb this one. There was no way I could do it, and David certainly couldn't haul me up that rock.

David took one look at the rock and decided to take an alternate route around the side of the peak. He was sure that we would find the trail on the other side.

Bad decision.

A quarter of the way around the peak, the rocks ran out. There was nowhere to walk except through thick growths of tiny evergreen trees. They were impossible to walk through. Every path we tried to take was a dead end.

I was exhausted. With no firm ground beneath my feet and shrubs gouging my sides with every step, I felt defeated. Each step I took felt like it had to be my last.

Dragging my body mere inches at a time through the thick brush was getting me nowhere. Why was I doing this? It just wasn't fun anymore. I was done.

Just as I had doubted my original decision to endure this hike, now I was doubting the wisdom of climbing this mountain. I couldn't go on. I fell to my side and breathed in deeply. David saw that I was struggling and pulled me to my feet. Lifting me by my pack handle, he urged me to move forward. I tried. I really did. But, my strength and my hiking spirit were gone.

I took a few steps and then fell to my side again.

"Let's go, Copper. We've got to get off this mountain. It's going to be getting dark soon."

I couldn't get up. Closing my eyes, I tried to visualize getting up and moving forward, taking a few steps at a time, with David urging me on.

"Copper, come on, get up! You can't rest now. We have to get off this mountain."

Again, I tried to make myself get up and again I failed.

Putting his hand on my pack and pulling me up to my feet, David said, "Come, Copper! Now!"

He let go of my pack and I fell to the ground.

After the fourth time of urging me forward, he realized I was not going anywhere. I was done. I was too physically and emotionally drained to go any further. The sun was nearly gone, the temperature was dropping fast, and I was really worried about how I was going to get down that mountain.

David saw the immediate danger and made a quick decision. "Copper, stay here. I'm going for help, and I'll be back soon. You stay, boy. I've got a plan."

I watched him head off down the side of the mountain. As soon as he was out of sight, I dragged myself to a higher flat rock so that I could see him as he went down, down, down the mountain. When he was out of sight, I made one more effort to get to my feet and follow him. It was no use. My legs were too weak.

Alone and cold, I knew that I'd never make it down the mountain. David was gone, there was no help in sight, David couldn't possibly get back before dark, and there was no way that he could carry me down the mountain. Especially in the dark.

After resigning myself to the fact that I would be spending the night on the mountain alone, I lay my head on the rock, and tried to sleep. The dimmer the twilight got, the colder the rocks became. There would be no sleep and there would be no food. It had been a long time since I'd been this scared. David had been gone a long time and I resigned myself to the fact that I would probably die on this mountain—alone.

I closed my eyes again and tried to remember the good times we had together. I wanted my last thoughts to be good ones. I wanted my thoughts to be of me and David frolicking in the woods back home without a care in the world. I wanted to remember him reading to me and telling me of the new adventures we'd take. I wanted to run, and swim, and... What was that clatter of pebbles falling down below? Was there someone there?

I took a sniff of the air and, YES! It was David! I could see him then, striding quickly up the mountain, barely visible in the fading twilight. He wasn't alone, either—he had brought someone to help.

As he knelt beside me to take my backpack off, he said, "Copper, this isn't going to be easy. I've emptied my backpack and I'm going to carry you down the mountain in it. It's going to feel a little scary for you, but you've got to trust me and my new friend here. He's the caretaker of the Grey Knob Cabin where we'll stay. He knows these mountains well.

"Remember when you felt a little scared as we tried out the canoe? Well, this is going to be like that. But you have to trust us."

I just lay there. I do trust David, but I was still scared because I was completely helpless.

David lowered his backpack to the ground, hoisted me up to his chest, and put me in tail first. I didn't like this at all and I wanted out! This was as bad as being trapped in that house during the thunderstorm. It was almost worse, since back then, I had the physical strength to burst through the screen door and run. This time I was trapped. There was no place for my feet to grip or for me to have any control of my own body. My tail was pinned under me and I had no way to keep my balance. All four feet were bound by the fabric of the backpack. I was panicking and I needed to get out!

As I continued to try to gain some balance and claw my way out, David kept calmly putting my legs and my body back in the pack and asking me to trust him. Finally, I gave in. I was too tired to fight anymore. I had to trust that David knew what he was doing.

He stuffed all 90 lbs. of me in the backpack, closed the drawstring loosely around my neck to secure it, lowered his body to the ground, put his arms through the straps and lifted me up on his back.

It wasn't comfortable at first and my weight and position pulled me away from David's back. I was tipping him over.

As I squirmed in fear, I felt David's new friend pushing on my body--up, down, left, and right--until I was leaning against David's back. I felt David take the first steps forward and I froze in fear.

While we moved slowly down the mountain, I could feel David slip and stumble in the dim light of twilight, each time being steadied by his friend and his hiking stick. It was a slow and arduous trip down the cold dark mountain.

When we finally made it safely to the cabin, I was eager to be let out of the backpack. David lowered his body to the ground, pulled off the pack and lay me carefully on the floor. He pulled me out of the pack and stroked my fur. It was over. David had somehow found the strength to bring me down off that mountain. I was exhausted. The caretaker made a bed for me and I silently thanked David as I drifted off to sleep on a soft warm blanket indoors and out of the cold. I couldn't even find the energy to give David a nose kiss to thank him. That would have to wait until tomorrow.

I awoke the next morning to hear David discussing my health and well-being with the caretaker of the cabin who had assisted David in my rescue. He had been such a huge help to David, and he could see that I was still in no shape to continue hiking.

"I have a friend down in Gorham who loves dogs, and she would take special care of Copper if you want him to stay with her for a few days," offered the caretaker. "Her name is Marium and she is the sweetest person you would ever want to meet. Copper might be a little spoiled after staying with her, but you won't have to worry about him getting good care. You could hike for a few days and then catch a ride back into town to pick him up."

"I don't really think I have a choice," said David. "He was really weak last night; he just can't continue hiking. I think I would like to give him some rest, consult his veterinarian, and then make a plan for him from there."

NO! PLEASE! I am so, so, sorry, David. I tried; I really did. Please don't leave me behind. I want to go with you.

"Ok, I'll call Marium," replied the caretaker.

We drove into Gorham, New Hampshire in the caretaker's truck. It was there that we met Marium for the first time.

"What a beautiful dog!" she said as we parked the truck in her yard. "What is this handsome dog's name?"

"This is Copper, and he's very tired and sore today," answered David.

Marium put her arms around my neck and said, "It's nice to meet you Copper. We are going to have fun the next few days. I'm going to brush you and bathe you, massage your tired muscles and spoil you rotten!"

David laughed, "He'll love that. Thank you so much for your help. Just let me know what I owe you for his care."

"Not one penny," exclaimed Marium. "It is my pleasure to care for this beautiful dog. You go ahead and enjoy your hike."

It was settled. I was being left behind.

David thanked her, hugged me goodbye and said, "I'm going to miss you buddy but you've got to let your body have time to heal. You be good now and do just what Marium says."

He gave me one final scratch behind the ears and said, "Rest well, buddy."

I was feeling very sad for many reasons as I watched David walk away. When we started the hike, I was so excited to go. I was full of courage and enthusiasm because I knew that David and I could conquer the Appalachian Trail together. David and I could do anything.

At that moment, I was beginning to realize that maybe I had to accept that I'm getting older, and I can't run and jump and climb like I once could.

I knew one thing for sure. I still loved David just as much as ever and I had a new respect for his love for me. He'd gone through a lot these last few months as he made sure I was safe and healthy. My questions remained, though. Should I have come? Would he have been better off if I'd stayed at home? I still wasn't sure.

Marium opened the door to her house and I went inside where she made good on her promises. She bathed me and brushed me, massaged my sore muscles, and generally spoiled me rotten. I spent my days at her house resting in the cool breeze outside, enjoying the sunshine, and enjoying her massages. She took great care of me while David hiked and climbed the Mahoosuc range. I walked too, but they were easy, slow walks in the backyard. It was a restful few days, but it just wasn't the same without David. He was out there on the trail continuing the adventure without me. It was supposed to be *our* adventure. I could only wonder if I would get to explore any more of the trail with him or if this was the end of the trail for me. He had given me one last chance to prove myself and I had blown it.

It had been four easy days at Marium's house when I caught a familiar scent and heard a voice saying, "Hey buddy! How's my Copper Head?"

I knew that voice! It was David's dad! He always called me Copper Head when he was teasing me or playing with me. How did he get here? How did he find me? He was supposed to be back in Georgia! I jumped up and walked over to find him smiling and laughing as he hugged me and roughed up my fur. Then he said, "Copper Head, you are going with me."

David's parents had been vacationing in New England and decided that they would like to hike short sections of the Appalachian Trail and visit the trail towns. They were driving towards New Hampshire when David called them to check in. He was surprised that they were arriving in New Hampshire and let them know that I was in Gorham taking a rest from the trail. David gave his parents Marium's phone number in case they wanted to check in on me. His mom called Marium to thank her and let her know that I would be traveling with them for a few days.

New Hampshire had been a tough state. I was sad that I wasn't hiking with David but glad that he was making miles. I would meet him in Maine in just a few more days. Right then, I was happy to be with the rest of my family as I waited to be reunited with David.

NORTHBOUNDERS
Notes from the Appalachian Trail in New Hampshire

- The White Mountains include the Presidential Range where the mountains are named after Presidents: Mt. Washington, Mt. Adams, Mt. Monroe, Mt. Jefferson, Mt. Eisenhower, and others.
- The White Mountains have weather that can change drastically by the minute.
- Mt. Washington is known for the worst weather on Earth.
- NEVER hike the White Mountains in bad weather or if there is even a *hint* of bad weather coming.
- A "notch," like Franconia Notch, is a gap or pass between two peaks.
- People in New Hampshire are very friendly and always willing to help.
- I love being part of a family that takes care of one another.
- Sometimes dreams have to be sacrificed for the sake of health.
- The Appalachian Trail through New Hampshire is about 151 miles
- We have walked 1,752 miles and completed 80% of the Appalachian Trail.

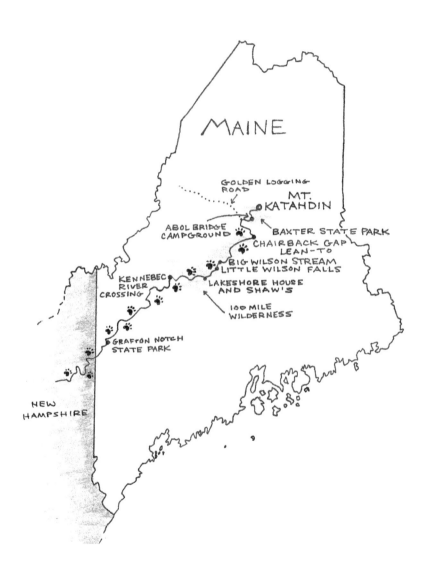

MAINE

GOLDEN LOGGING
ROAD

MT.
KATAHDIN

ABOL BRIDGE
CAMPGROUND

BAXTER STATE PARK

CHAIRBACK GAP
LEAN-TO

BIG WILSON STREAM
LITTLE WILSON FALLS

KENNEBEC
RIVER
CROSSING

LAKESHORE HOUSE
AND SHAW'S

100 MILE
WILDERNESS

GRAFTON NOTCH
STATE PARK

NEW
HAMPSHIRE

CHAPTER 17
Maneuvering Through Maine

When David left to continue the hike without me, he had planned for us to meet up again at Grafton State Park in Maine. As we traveled through New Hampshire and on into Maine, there was much continuous discussion between David's mom and dad about my continuing on the trail.

"There is no way he can hike anymore. He's too old to be hiking this kind of terrain. It's tough out here. I'm just going to tell David that it's over. Copper is done," said David's dad clenching his jaw.

"Let's just see how he does in the next few days. He's come this far and it might just be that he needs a long rest," countered David's mom.

"No, he's done. A 70-year-old man wouldn't be hiking the Appalachian Trail, and I'm not going to watch him suffer as he tries to finish. Copper's 10 dog years equate to a man of 70 years!"

David's dad was serious. He rubbed me gently and hugged my neck. I knew how much he loved me, and he didn't want to see me hurting. And I had to admit the possibility that he was right, even as I hoped that maybe I'd be allowed to hike at least a little bit more of the trail.

"I've been doing a lot of reading about the hikers on the trail this year," said David's mom. "Right now, there are two sisters on the trail. One is 82 years old, and the other is 83. There's also a 74 year old man on the trail. All of them, when interviewed, say they take the trail one day at a time, rest when they become tired, and then head out again when they are ready. They follow the same pattern of hike, rest, hike, rest, and let their bodies be their guide. Maybe that's what Copper needs, a good rest."

"No," answered David's dad. "Copper's done."

I didn't like that. I didn't want to be done. I wanted to rest and then hike some more. I had a week before we would see David again and hoped I could convince his dad otherwise by then.

As we traveled in the car, I slept soundly. When we stopped at night to sleep, I continued my routine of a short walk with David's mom before bed and a short walk in the morning. We continued that routine for five days. By the fifth day, I was feeling strong.

David's dad drove to Grafton State Park to pick up David as he came out of the woods at the trailhead. As soon as we got there, I could smell the hikers. I bounded out of the car and ran straight toward the trailhead. David's mom let out a laugh, "Did you see how he just leapt out of the car and ran straight to the trail? Now *that* doesn't look like a 70-year-old man to me! How did he know where the trail was? I certainly couldn't see it from here."

It really isn't that hard to find when you've been hiking it for months. Besides, the hiker scent is very strong. They are smelly because they hike for days without a shower or change of clothes. There are no showers or washing machines in the woods. They clean up the best they can with the water they have, but with all the sweating, it's just not possible to smell good.

I lay down at the trailhead and waited for what felt like hours. Just as I drifted off to sleep, I smelled him. I caught David's scent a mile away. I jumped up and ran into the woods with David's mom right behind me. I ran and ran until I saw him sauntering down the mountain humming a little tune. David immediately picked up his pace until he reached me and then fell to his knees as he grabbed me in a welcome embrace. David was back, the family was together, and I was getting stronger and healthier every day.

David's dad had not seen his son for many months and they reunited with lots of hugs, slaps on the back, and comments like, "You look good, buddy!" "You're so thin!" and "It's good to see you...but I wish I didn't have to smell you." They laughed together and walked side by side to the car.

When we got in the car, I jumped in the back seat with David and laid my head across his lap just to be near him. We had to drive with the windows down because his parents didn't want to be trapped in a closed vehicle with that hiker smell, so they let down all the windows in the car. David was pretty cold and shivering from the cool wind coming through the windows on his sweat-soaked clothing. That just gave him more reason to snuggle with me. I don't mind the smell. He just smells like David the hiker. He certainly smells better than that skunk back in New Jersey!

We all slept well that night, and the next morning, David's family made a plan. David would slackpack a short section of the A.T., and he invited his mom to hike with him. She was excited because it included a canoe ride across the Kennebec River. (Yes, a canoe ride is actually part of the Appalachian Trail and the canoe has a white blaze in it to prove it.) I stayed back and spent time with David's dad in hopes that he would begin to see that I was strong again. I was really missing my hiking time with David, but I knew that I had to show my strength if I had any chance of getting back on the trail. So far, David's dad was adamant about the fact that I was done hiking. He was not swayed by any of David's or David's mom's arguments.

Day after day, David hiked the trail. Day after day, I was not allowed to go.

I did get to see some of the hikers when we'd stay at hiker hostels. We stayed at Lakeshore House one night and had breakfast at Shaw's Hiker Hostel the next morning where we saw Dangerpants, Speck, and several other hikers we had met along the trail. They were eager to be finishing the trail and very happy to see me, but were sad to hear that I was no longer hiking. Needless to say, I got lots of hugs, roughhousing, ear scratches and smiles from them. They also encouraged me to get better so we could hike on the trail together again before we all went home.

I think David's dad must have been listening to my hiker friends because that night, David and his dad finally had a discussion that sounded promising.

David was about to start on a section of the trail called the "100 Mile Wilderness." There are no towns for a hundred miles of trail, so you must take everything you will need for seven days.

As they were discussing the hike, David said, "Dad, I really think Copper is ready to hike again. Do you see how he runs and plays? And, every time I start down a trail, he's eager to come with me. He's trying to tell us that he's ready." He turned to me and said, "Isn't that right, Copper?"

I pranced and turned in circles when David asked the question. As a final plea for permission, I let out a loud bark, put my paw squarely on his dad's thigh, and looked pleadingly into his eyes.

His dad shook his head and said, "No, David, he's not ready."

At that comment, I gave an even louder bark, ran back and forth to the door, barked again, and once again looked pleadingly into his eyes hoping he could see how desperately I wanted to go back to the trail.

He looked back at me and said, hesitantly, "Okay, Copper Head. I don't like it,, but if you're that confident, I guess I'll give you another chance."

Yes! Finally! Thank You! Load me up with food, and I'll prove how strong I am.

I slept restlessly that night and couldn't wait to get back on the trail. At sunrise, David strapped on my pack. I felt strong and eager to see more of the A.T. We set off into the woods before noon. We hiked steadily that day, and it seemed like David was happy to have me with him again.

When we stopped at North Pond to take a picture, David reminisced about our time together.

"I sure do wish we had a canoe so we could take a ride across the pond, don't you, Copper?"

I do too, David. That was a good adventure.

I think he understood how much I wanted to be with him.

Soon we came upon Little Wilson Falls. David knows I don't like to cross through water so deep that I can't see the bottom and generally lets me scout out a place that I feel safe to cross. But this time, David was very particular about where and how we crossed. He seemed very concerned about this crossing.

"Okay, Copper, to ford this stream we are going to cross right next to this rope that someone has run across the creek. I'm going to need you to do exactly as I say. I'm going to keep you on the upstream side of me, you lean into me, and I'm going to hold onto the rope to keep us both from being washed downstream."

We stepped into the cold roaring stream and I immediately felt the pull of the water. The current was too strong, and I was losing my balance. My pack was pulling me sideways, pushing me up and away from David. I could feel myself sliding and being pulled by the water. Then, I realized that a strong force was pulling me back. As I glanced to the side, I saw David's big hand holding tightly to the top of my pack. He was balancing himself on the rocks while the water slammed forcefully into our legs.

"Lean in, Copper," he yelled as he pulled me toward him. "Lean towards my legs."

He managed to keep one hand on me and one hand on the rope as I did my best to lean towards his legs and keep us both in step together as we forded the stream. Finally, we reached solid ground. He had kept his promise. We had made it safely to the other side.

"That was a tough one," said David. "I sure am glad someone tied that rope across the stream. The water is so strong it would have swept us away. And, you did great, boy. You stayed right by my side and did exactly the right thing. Good boy!"

Little did he know, I had no choice. I had to walk alongside him just to keep from floating down the creek to who-knows-where. Whoever named this Little Wilson Falls needs to examine the meaning of the word "*little*".

Before we knew it, we were at Big Wilson stream. This meant another ford across the stream, another rope to hold tightly to, and another hope that we made it across. This time the water was much shallower and less forceful, so it was easier to cross.

Someone got their words mixed up. Little Wilson Creek was a big scary stream crossing, and Big Wilson was a tame, little stream crossing. Strange!

The weather had been nice since we started the 100-Mile Wilderness, but I could tell by the air that things were about to change. I can smell rain and sense thunder long before humans have any idea that it is on the way.

The rain held off long enough for us to make it to Chairback Gap Lean-to where I met some of David's new friends that he made while I stayed behind at Chet's House. Counselor, Wonder Boy, and Piper were already there when we arrived, and David took time to introduce me to them.

Just as he finished the introductions and jumped into the lean-to, it began to rain.

"Bring Copper up here in this shelter," said Wonder Boy. "There's only four of us here tonight, and there is no reason that he should have to sleep in the rain and mud."

"Yeah," said Piper. "He's hiked just as hard and long as the rest of us."

"And, if he is anything like my Golden Retriever," said Counselor, "he's not particularly fond of thunder and lightning."

It was nice of them to invite me into the shelter because it was a very stormy night. The crawlspace under the sleeping platform made an excellent hiding place from the storm's wrath, which I admit, still scared me a bit.

As the hikers talked on into the night, I found myself getting very sleepy. I had made it this far into the 100-Mile Wilderness and I was not going to let David down. I needed my rest so that I would be ready to go in the morning. I needn't have worried though. Morning came with more rain, thunder, and lightning. David decided that we weren't going anywhere.

When the sun came out later in the day, David put on his pack and strapped mine onto me. We set off for several more days of walking through the 100-Mile Wilderness without any real problems. There were the huge mud puddles filling the trail along the way, trees blocking the trail with no way over or under, the usual stream crossings, and the tired legs from walking, but, all in all, we had a good trip. David and I kept to the schedule he had set and we finished the 100-Mile Wilderness in seven days as planned.

David had asked his parents to meet us at Abol Bridge Campground where the trail comes out of the woods and onto the Golden Road. When we crossed the bog bridge that let David know we were getting close, he said "We're almost there, Copper. You made it! I can't wait for Dad to see how healthy you look and watch you come out of these woods."

When I saw David's parent's car, I started running. I wanted his dad to see that I had made it through the 100-Mile Wilderness and was still eager to be hiking.

David's dad got out of the car and said, "Well, look who's running down the trail. Is it Copper Head?"

I loved it when he called me that! I ran straight ahead into his arms and into a big hug and my favorite scratches behind the ears. I had made it through the 100 Mile Wilderness!

The end of the Appalachian Trail for most northbound hikers is the climb up Mt. Katahdin in Baxter State Park. When David and I came out of the wilderness, we could see Mt. Katahdin in the distance. It was a huge mountain and I wanted to climb it with David and go all the way to the end of the Appalachian Trail.

But I couldn't. Dogs are not allowed in Baxter State Park or on Mt. Katahdin.

The best I could do was to gaze up at it as we traveled down the Golden Road. David would sleep one last time in Maine before he reached the end of the trail in the North by climbing Mt. Katahdin.

Just like in the Smoky Mountains, I would be left behind not because I *couldn't* climb, but rather because I wasn't *allowed* to climb.

David set out the next morning to fulfill his dream. He started at sunrise to climb the Abol Trail to the top. I was so excited for him, but, I was sad that I couldn't be by his side when he reached the top. I wanted to celebrate with him and have our picture made at the top with the sign he had showed me that said simply: KATAHDIN.

"Don't worry, buddy," he had said. "I'll carry a picture of you all the way to the top. You're my hiking buddy, and your spirit will be with me all the way."

And he did. My picture went to the top with him. We had climbed Katahdin together.

Notes from the Appalachian Trail in Maine

- There are lots of roots and rocks and stream crossings in Maine.
- A lean-to in Maine is another name for a shelter for hikers.
- The 100-mile wilderness is not difficult to hike if you have enough food.
- Dogs are not allowed in Baxter State Park or on Mt. Katahdin.
- The Mahoosuc Notch is often called the toughest, but most fun mile on the Appalachian Trail.
- The Appalachian Trail through Maine is about 282 miles.
- David has walked 1,804 miles and completed 83% of the trail.

TENNESSEE
NORTH
CAROLINA
BLOOD MOUNTAIN
WOODS HOLE
SPRINGER
MOUNTAIN
AMICALOLA
FALLS
SNELLVILLE
GEORGIA

CHAPTER 18
Getting Back to Georgia

After David conquered Katahdin and finished up a few sections in Maine he had missed, we had a long drive south to get to North Carolina, so we could hike back home to Georgia. Two days and over a thousand miles later, we arrived at Fontana Village, North Carolina. We were well-rested and eager to complete our flip-flop thru-hike.

David said, "These last 165 miles are going to be a breeze, Copper. We've already done the hardest part."

That first day was a big mile day, and I handled it like a pro. It seemed that the long rest on the ride from Maine to North Carolina had given my body time to recover. I was proud of myself. David was right about it being an easy hike, but he forgot about the weather. With winter coming on again, the North Carolina mountains were rapidly getting colder. I found myself almost wishing for the heat of summer in spite of the warm, fur coat I always wear.

We found a shelter as night fell, and David rolled out his pad and sleeping bag. There was no one else around, so he invited me in, tucked me under his legs to keep me warm, and fell fast asleep. We slept well that night, even in the cold. In the morning, David could see that I was shivering, so he hopped out of his sleeping bag, tucked me into it, and ran off to get water to cook breakfast. It was so warm inside the bag that I drifted off to sleep.

When the sun warmed us up, David said, "Let's go buddy, we've got some hiking to do". It was a beautiful day out on the trail and our bodies warmed up quickly as we hiked. David was silent for much of the walk and finally spoke when we came upon a natural wonder.

"Here we are, Copper. That giant hole with the river running through it is the Nantahala Gorge. Those mountains go up 5,000 feet on either side of the river which eventually dumps into Fontana Lake. Isn't it beautiful?"

As he rubbed my head and looked into my panic stricken eyes, he said, "Yep, we have to climb into and out of it. But, the good news is that there will be a special treat waiting for you at the bottom."

We descended into the gorge, and when we reached the bottom, David went inside a building and came out with--a hamburger patty!

My special treat! I devoured it in a heartbeat. Spirits high, we hiked the long slow climb back out of the gorge.

The rest of the trail was easy on us as we made our way through North Carolina. It stayed smooth and level until we reached Standing Indian Mountain, the highest peak on the Appalachian Trail south of the Smoky Mountains. It is actually taller than Mt. Katahdin. We were both in good shape, so we tackled it with our usual fervor and made it to the top in record time. We kept this pace up for two more days of gorgeous weather, and just like that, we were crossing the border back into our home state. Home sweet home. Georgia!

Unfortunately, the pleasant weather did not remain for our hiking finale. The clouds got darker, and I could feel a storm coming. It was moving in fast. My fur became electrified and every bone in my body was screaming, *DANGER!* David knew I wasn't liking the looks of things and said, "Alright buddy, we've got four miles to hike over Blood Mountain to get to Woods Hole Shelter. We'll have a nice dry place to sleep if we can make it over the toughest mountain in Georgia. I know you're nervous about this storm, but I need you to bring out that hiker spirit and brave the storm one last time."

I talked myself into remaining somewhat calm even though many times I just wanted to bolt. David wasn't liking the storm either. I think the pep talk was just as much for himself as it was for me. Nobody likes climbing mountains in a thunderstorm. We left in a hurry and climbed Blood Mountain as quickly as we could. The rain was coming down hard and we had to endure a tough climb over slippery rocks, pouring rain, and that incessant thunder.

When we arrived at the top, David said, "No more walking, Copper. We're staying right here at Blood Mountain Shelter. I've had enough rain and storm for one night. I'm proud of you, buddy. You stayed right by my side through the entire thunderstorm. You never once tried to run. I think you have done it, Copper—you have conquered your fear of thunderstorms and proven your loyalty. This calls for a special dinner and double treats!"

What a day. I *had* conquered my fear and made it through a horrific thunderstorm without running away. I still didn't like them, but I felt stronger and proud for having faced my fear.

David dried me off with a towel and then motioned me into the strong, rock shelter we would have to ourselves that night. David cooked a special rice and beef dinner—one of my favorites—which we shared. We curled ourselves together for warmth as we bedded down for the night. After hiking so hard, we slept very well.

We enjoyed two more days of hiking with starts before sunrise. We had met only a few people on the trail for much of our southbound portion of the hike because it was nearing November, and few people hike the A.T. in winter months. The third morning after Blood Mountain, David seemed in no hurry to get out of camp. He also seemed really happy. In fact, when we were finally on our way, he was singing and bounding all the way down the trail.

Eventually, he deigned to tell me why: "Copper, old boy, we're not finishing the trail today even though we could. There's going to be a big *Welcome Home* party at one of the cabins at Amicalola Falls tonight, and many of our friends and family will be there. They are all coming to celebrate the end of the hike with us. Tonight we'll eat lots of good food, see people we haven't seen in a while, and enjoy a big campfire out back. Tomorrow, our friends and family will hike the last mile with us to the top of Springer Mountain, where the A.T. *begins* for most thru-hikers, but where it *ends* for us. It's been a good hike, hasn't it old boy?"

We had made it.

He pulled me close, gave me a big hug, and then made me chase him down to the Springer Mountain trailhead where David's mom met us and drove us to the cabin.

We arrived before most of the guests and David's little sister, Mikella, was the first one to greet us. She hadn't seen her brother in six months.

She grabbed David, gave him a big hug, and then said, "*Ewwwww, you stink!*"

David let out a belly laugh, pulled her even tighter for a longer hug, gave her a playful punch in the arm, and said, "I'm on my way to the shower now."

"Hurry up," she said. "I'm going to need a shower too, now that you've gotten that stink all over me."

David left for the shower and Mikella turned to me and said, "Look up here on the wall, Copper. This banner says, *Congratulations Blast and Copper! Appalachian Trail thru-hikers. 2,186 miles.* That's for you! You did it, you hiked the Appalachian Trail with my brother. Well, you still have to hike another mile tomorrow, but you're almost through."

She gave me a big hug and a smile. I had missed her.

David had just enough time to get a shower before everyone arrived. Then, the congratulations and hugging and hand shaking began.

There were a lot of guests who came to celebrate and they were eager to get a picture with me and David under the six foot congratulations sign above the table filled with food for all.

My favorite guests who came to celebrate were the children: Aidan, Evan, Kaylynn, and Rebekkah. They kept me company, played with me, and gave me lots of hugs and belly rubs. Then they gave me dog treats to celebrate!

As the guests gathered outside by the fire to talk and hear all about our hike, I fell soundly asleep, and I'm sure I did a round or two of snoring.

After a big breakfast the next morning, it was time to hike the final mile. All of our family and friends who had come to celebrate walked straight up Springer Mountain in a long line of celebration. Aidan, age 2, was the youngest hiker to celebrate our seven month hike and the oldest guest in the line was David's dad at 60 years old.

As David and I reached the top of Springer Mountain, he pulled me in close for a hug and whispered in my ear, "We did it boy; we did it together!"

He had a big smile on his face and raised his arms high in the air. He had walked 2,186 miles, the entire Appalachian Trail, and I had done most of it with him.

Cheers went up from family and friends, as well as strangers who were hiking Springer Mountain that beautiful November day. The strangers were snapping pictures and asking questions about our adventure. They couldn't believe that they had met two Appalachian Trail hikers who had walked the entire trail between Georgia and Maine. Some of them shared hopes of one day accomplishing the goal for themselves. They raised bottles of water in a toast to the man and dog who were celebrities that day on Springer Mountain.

There were only three things left to do with family, friends and strangers looking on.

First, David signed the trail journal stowed at the top of Springer Mountain with our names, "Blast and Copper" and put my paw print right beside it.

Second, David's mom took a picture of us together with the Appalachian Trail plaque on the top of Springer, which marked the end point of our Appalachian Trail hike.

The last thing—well, you may already have guessed.

David ate an entire cake to signify finishing the entire trail! It took him awhile, but he did it with all of his friends and family cheering him on. The Appalachian Trail thru-hike was completed, and he had an empty cake plate to prove it.

Well, he didn't actually eat the *whole* cake, he gave me the last bite which I took right from his lips.

As we made our way down the mountain and I listened to the hum of family and friends chatting and celebrating, I had only one thought in my mind. What would be our next hiking adventure? I couldn't wait to find out.

We walked silently, side by side, down the mountain together.

Blast and Copper—forever hiking buddies—forever friends.

Final Notes from the Appalachian Trail

- Georgia has gorgeous mountain vistas.
- The Appalachian Trail through Georgia is about 79 miles.
- Celebrating with family and friends (and even strangers) was a perfect way to end our hike.
- David has walked 2,186 miles and 100% of the trail.
- David is the best friend and hiking buddy anyone could ever have!
- In the end, it was more important to me that I proved I was a true and loyal friend, even if I couldn't hike all 2,186 miles of the Trail. Having David's friendship is worth it all.

Afterword

There would not be another grand adventure for Copper in this lifetime. He came home healthy and strong and enjoyed hiking in the woods with David on short day and weekend hikes for two more years. In the end, heart cancer took this beautiful soul's life.

Copper left this Earth on a warm and sunny spring day in March just five days before David's birthday. He died in David's arms while enjoying belly rubs and much loved ear scratches as he took his last breath.

A more beautiful, loved, and well-mannered Golden Retriever has never lived. Copper left over 10,000,000 paw prints on the 2,186 mile trail giving friendship to all those he met while enduring almost every dramatic scene set in this story.

An indelible paw print will remain on the heart of David, his number one fan, the planner of their adventures, the Appalachian Trail thru-hiker, and Copper's very best friend.

Forever loved, forever missed, and forever remembered: Copper, the hiking dog.

Acknowledgments

Just as this was Copper's first adventure on the Appalachian Trail, this was my first adventure in authorship. The journey was arduous, just as Copper's journey was, but we both learned a great deal along the way and had special people surrounding us who made the journey possible.

The biggest thank you goes to my son, David, a talented writer who tirelessly and enthusiastically read and edited this manuscript many times. Because he *lived* the journey with Copper, he pushed me to dig deeper, feel more, and expand scenes, to find Copper's voice and engage the reader in the difficulty, excitement, joy and pain of hiking the Appalachian Trail. His friendship and loyalty to Copper was the same friendship and loyalty that he gave to me as I pursued this new endeavor. I cannot thank him enough.

Other family members also contributed to the book and I am appreciative of their time and talent. My daughter, Mikella, gave me the inspiration for the title and for the design of the book cover. My husband, Mike, took her idea, and created the artwork needed for submission to the artist in completing the cover.

Thank you to the illustrator, Nathaniel Hinton, who took the words on the page and turned them into drawings that made me smile. He was patient and professional as he captured Copper in his finest moments.

Thank you to Christina Yother, who first mentored me in the process of writing and was willing to give the first harsh critique to encourage me to find Copper's best story in the words.

Thank you to Danny Woodard, who created the first mock-up of the design for the cover to help me understand the design process.

Thank you to Jovana Shirley of Unforeseen Editing for answering question after question as I stumbled my way through the publishing process. Her answers kept me on track.

Thank you to Najla Qambar of Najla Qambar Designs for the final book cover. Her patience and attention to detail are greatly appreciated.

The final acknowledgement is for all the people along the Appalachian Trail who assisted Copper in his journey. The world is full of compassionate and unselfish people. I hope you enjoy reading about your kindness in the covers of this book. Copper's journey would not have been possible without you.

About the Author

Dr. Karen Lord Rutter is a retired teacher and administrator with over 30 years in education whose work with students ranged from preschool through high school. Dr. Rutter has a passion for travel, children, and learning. This book was inspired when her son, David, thru-hiked the Appalachian Trail with the family dog, Copper. Her love of the Appalachian Trail was born after David invited her to hike a few short sections of the A.T. with him. Because of her passion for children and love of reading, she embarked upon her first foray into the world of writing for children. As an educator, it was important that she incorporate history, geography, enriched vocabulary, science, and math into Copper's story.

Dr. Rutter is a lifelong resident of Georgia, where the Appalachian Trail begins. She and her husband, Mike, have two adult children: David, who edited this story, and Mikella, who inspired the cover art and title. This book is a labor of love for a pet who left the family much too soon.